Llooped

Samson McCune

Copyright © 2024 McCune Entertainment LLC

ISBN-13: 978-1-958401-02-6

Cover art by Samson McCune
Interior design by Samson McCune

Give feedback on the book at:
samsonmccune@gmail.com

First Edition

Printed in the U.S.A

For those that feel as if they've been left behind.

Contents:

Art:

Dawn

A heavy weight settled upon the man as he became aware. His name was Leo. He was lost. What else did he know other than loss? It was hard to understand. His head pounded and his chest burned. He lay his hand on the heat and a vague sense of déjà vu washed over him.

With effort he rose to his feet, breaking free from a thin prison of snow. It must have fallen on him as he was sleeping.

Sleeping.

Leo furrowed his brow and started on his way, moving with deliberation that didn't match how he felt.

Where was he?

He stumbled through the darkness of an unfamiliar icy forest. It was still the middle of the night, and he was quickly regretting how quick he had been to leave his camp. Had he left anything behind? Would it have been wise to go back to sleep until the sun had risen?

When he stepped on a sharp stick that had been hidden by the snow, he became acutely aware of his lack of foot protection. An old pair of thin socks were his only defense against inevitable frostbite.

Slowly, the thin veil of fog that had been plaguing his thoughts began to clear, and some sense returned to his confused mind. He was searching for the a magical land of unknown properties—the only place he knew of where he could get the answers he desired. A god had told him about it. Of it, he knew little, but hope fueled his desires, and he searched for it anyway.

It bothered Leo that it had taken so long for him to remember that. A broken body was one thing, but a broken mind was another altogether. He wasn't sure if he would be able to handle a life without clarity.

A realization flashed through his mind. That's why he had become a journalist in the first place. More than anything, he had always been motivated by truth and justice. And now that the world was dead and gone, he needed to discover why. He needed to uncover the truth behind the most egregious sin in history.

Somehow.

Vaguely, loss tugged at his mind, but Leo pushed it away. Everything was gone. Of course he was upset. There was no use focusing on it now.

As he walked, the horizon began to glow, melting away some of the numbness that had been crystalizing in his mind. Like a moth to a flame, he stumbled forwards, eager for the morning and the warmth it offered.

How long had it been since he had last seen a blue sky and felt the tender love of sunshine? He could almost hear the songs of spring in his mind. One bird in particular was louder than the rest, and there was something else, too. Was it laughter?

When he tried to focus on the sounds, the memory faded and he was alone once more. All that was left was that pesky sense of loss that seemed to be infecting his mind.

But one other thing caught his attention during his trek, and he couldn't quite place why. That particular forest, in that particular moment, was far too silent, too still, for his liking. Now all he could see was fresh snow and hear the loudness of the silent wood through the whispering gusts of wind.

There were no animals.

A wolf howled in the distance.

Well, maybe there were some.

With a shiver, Leo hugged his body and forced himself to keep moving forward, certain of only that he had a long journey ahead of him.

Llooped

Midday hung overhead like a long forgotten friend, but even its kindness couldn't pierce the shadows that filled both Leo's mind and the forest. Frost clung to his beard, and his feet glowed with false warmth. Time was running out. He needed to find shelter, and fast.

As the sun climbed higher into the sky, the world began to weep, its tears falling onto Leo as he tread through the snow. The brightness of the sun was almost enough to blind him, to deter him from the path that he felt somehow was true. It obscured the draw of the horizon, telling him that maybe light and comfort didn't have to be so far away.

But the sun lied, even its divinity not too far-removed from the base instincts of the lesser beings that Leo knew he had studied. Even it spoke in hushed tones and sugary sentences to pull him away from his goal.

The horizon still called his name.

So further Leo trudged, maintaining his misunderstood determination. It was as if he were being pulled along by some strange force, whether it be fate or instinct. Regardless of its origin, this power dragged him through the forest, keeping him from death and filling him with hope.

The brightness of the sun faded as a cloud passed overhead. Leo looked up to investigate and grit his teeth with frustration. Somehow, he knew this to be a stratus cloud, and that meant precipitation. In a warmer environment, that would have meant rain, but here in the depths of an ice forest, it likely meant snow.

More importantly, though, his one solace from the cold was gone. He had no idea how long the sun would be obstructed by the clouds but hoped that it wouldn't be long.

It took a minute for his eyes to adjust from the searing bright white light that had come before to the gray darkness that had permeated the wood. It was as if the world had flipped completely, all that had been bright was now dark, and all that had brought warmth now brought cold.

Leo could feel his hope wilting. It wasn't dead, nor was it dying. Rather it was a flower in a storm, strong and aware. A challenge had arrived.

The thickening forest stood as an indomitable foe, one built to crush Leo. Its teeth were the fallen branches whose broken wood was as sharp as a razor. Its skin was the rock and ice that formed the ground. With a deafening roar, wind rushed out of the beast's mouth and slammed into his face. The cold stung.

But even against such a terrifying enemy, Leo stood tall and continued onward. There was no beast, not really. The true battle he was fighting was internal, with despair as his only opposition. So all he had to do to win was to keep going, to keep walking even when his body didn't recognize itself anymore. That was all.

Just keep walking.

Deeper into the beast's mouth he walked, struggling to convince himself that walking was truly his only recourse. His destination was becoming muddled with each step. Pain closed around him, constructing his tomb.

Death was near and certain.

Had despair won?

Leo took a few more steps, knowing that he was going to stop soon. Snow had begun to fall from the sky, its shroud unwelcome. Each step taunted him, begging to be his last. His feet screamed in agony as the frostbrite crawled up his legs.

He wasn't quite sure what drove him to ignore the cries. Something within him wouldn't let him quit, wouldn't let him succumb to the beast.

And then, just when he thought this last, unbreakable part of him was going to give in, too, he saw it.

At first it was so pale and dim that Leo thought himself to be hallucinating. Confused, he stumbled closer to verify, and sure enough, there it was, the orange glow of a flame on the end of a stick. A torch had been stuck into the ground, serving to save any lost soul that might get lost enough to need it.

Grinning, Leo rushed towards the fire. He could hardly wait to feel the warmth that the fire was sure to bring. When he arrived, it took all of his willpower not to throw himself on top of it. Was there a way for him to wrap his cloak around it to trap more heat? Not without burning himself, he couldn't imagine. So instead he stood as close as possible without hurting himself and tried to let the heat envelop his body.

Only now, with the flame so close to him, was Leo able to recognize just how frozen his body had become and just how near to death he was.

"I hope you have a long life, friend," Leo said with a chuckle, distantly aware of the fact that it was the first time he had spoken in recent memory. His words felt dull and cluttered, and his voice sounded weird out loud.

"If we make it through this, maybe I can take the time to practice talking more," he mused.

He half expected the torch to reply.

The heat was his companion, but the same as all of his late friends, it too had to leave soon. And soon was sooner than he had expected. A gust of wind blew through the forest and the torch went out with a puff.

Darkness flooded Leo's vision.

He blinked back the shadows and coughed as he inhaled a cloud of smoke. His eyes watered and stung. When they cleared, he found another orange glow, deeper in the forest this time.

His heart leaped. Was it another torch? This time he would protect it from the wind and hold onto it as long as he could. This time, he wouldn't make the same mistake as before. This time, he wouldn't let it go.

In an exhausted daze, Leo stumbled towards the glow. He counted his steps, hoping that it would give him the strength to go on. His body was barely working, but he only needed it to hold out for a bit longer. Soon, he would be warm again.

He got closer and found that he was wrong. It wasn't a torch. It was something far more magnificent. The sound of his footsteps on the wooden stairs echoed through the air triumphantly. Leo smiled and reached an arm out towards the cabin. He could only imagine the comfort and safety inside. All he needed to do was

"Warmth"

knock.

He passed out with his hand an inch from the door.

| | |

Leo groaned and sat up, pushing a heavy blanket off of him as he did. His body felt tight and tingled as if he had been poked by thousands of small needles. He rubbed his eyes and looked around, trying to remember where he was and what had happened.

He sat near the fireplace inside a log cabin. A few animal heads had been placed as trophies along the walls, and there was a rifle on display on top of the mantle, but otherwise the house was sparse with decoration. There was hardly any furniture either. Presently, he sat on a pile of animal skins.

The front door swung open, and in marched a large man. He had a bushy beard and thick, tattoo-covered arms. Essentially, he looked like the stereotypical lumberjack, and given the firewood in his arms, Leo would not have been surprised to learn that this was, in fact, his occupation.

"How was your nap?" the man grumbled.

It took Leo a moment to realize that he was being addressed.

"You brought me in?" Leo replied.

The man shrugged. "It wouldn't have been right to leave a man to freeze on my very porch." He dropped the firewood on the ground next to the fireplace and then brushed his hands on his pants as he sat beside Leo and admired the hearth. It was dying down a bit, so the lumberjack-looking fellow reached over and tossed another log in, sending embers into the air.

"My name is Hank, by the way," the newcomer said after they listened to the fire crackle and pop for a few minutes. "I've been living out here by myself for a while, so I was a bit surprised to see you yesterday. I hope you're feeling better after getting some rest. Hypothermia and frostbite are both far too familiar these days."

"I'm Leo," Leo replied, though as the words left his mouth,

they carried the bad taste that only followed from an untruth. It wasn't a lie, not necessarily, but he couldn't remember the truth. So Leo would have to do.

He suddenly found it strange that he couldn't remember where he had gotten the name.

"How did you end up in this neck of the woods?" Hank asked quizzically. "The closest settlement to here is a small village a couple miles north, but I haven't seen or heard from them in a long time. Were you trying to find them?"

Leo tried to recall which way he had been going before finding Hank's cabin. Had it been north? The sun was purely a beacon of light in his memory, its location obscured.

"I'm following fate," Leo said honestly. "If that happens to take me to the settlement to the north, then that's where I'll be going."

Hank smiled. "I admire that. Complete faith. I haven't seen someone with that kind of conviction since the world broke."

Leo's face brightened. It hadn't occurred to him that someone might be able to give him the answers that he was looking for. "You know what happened to the world? You remember why it broke?"

Hank's face darkened and the fire began to die once more. Leo reached over to grab a piece of wood to keep it going, but the lumberjack stopped him with a firm shake of his head before he could.

"Of course, I do," he replied. "Everybody does. Doesn't mean I want to talk about it."

Leo poked and prodded at his lumberjack companion a few more times, trying his best to reignite their conversation, but Hank was clearly uninterested. One-word replies were all he gave until they went to bed as the moon rose and the world was blanketed in darkness. Undeterred, Leo resolved to ask again in the morning, though he could tell that Hank was, if anything, true to his word.

|

With a bang, the front door exploded into splinters, shattering Leo's world of dreams. He shot to his feet, eyes darting around the room to see what had happened. The door had shot inwards, meaning someone was breaking in.

But who? Or what?

A second later, three men rushed into the room, wielding dangerous-looking rifles in full-body armor. Their faces were obscured by tinted visors.

Leo shot his hands in the air. "I'm unarmed," he yelled, suddenly acutely aware of his pounding heart.

The intruders ignored him.

Leo looked around the room, and other than the three men and their rifles, he realized that he was alone. Where was Hank? And what were the intruders doing there?

With a thump, one of the riflemen dropped like a rock. The other two panicked, breaking what Leo could now recognize as a formation, and searched frantically for what had attacked their third.

In the darkness, Leo thought he could see the gleam of steel near the fallen man's neck, but the light was too low to be sure. A moment later another man fell much the same as the first, leaving only one more rifleman standing.

"Fucking hell, Hank. Stop it. Please," the man shouted, not trying to hide the urgency in his face. "We just came to talk."

Leo scoffed. With rifles? It took a great deal of willpower for him not to give the intruder a piece of his mind, especially for ruining a night of fitful sleep. He rose to his feet and eyed the rifleman.

"You there," the rifleman called over to Leo, apparently just noticing him. "Are you a friend of Hank's?"

Leo took a step towards the intruder and an instant later was looking down the barrel of a gun. "I came here yesterday," Leo said easily. "Or maybe the day before. Either way, I haven't been here long."

He took another step towards the intruder, testing to see how far he could go.

"Listen to me," the rifleman said, his voice wavering, "you need to get out of here. It isn't safe."

"I've enjoyed my time here," Leo countered. "I doubt I'd be alive if it weren't for Hank."

The rifleman sighed and his hand started to shake slightly. "Just because he did something good doesn't mean that he's a good man. Please, for your own sake, I need you to trust me on this."

Leo briefly wondered why the third of the intruders was still standing unlike the others and then returned his attention to the gun pointed at his head. He took another careful step forward.

"And I should trust you instead of the man that saved my life? You, who threatens me with violence?"

The rifleman seemed to consider this, and lowered the gun halfway, then raised it once more after Leo took another step forward. He was almost within arm's reach. Maybe then he could get around the barrel of the gun. If he was learning one thing these days it was to get ahead of problems before they became too big to handle.

"Stop right there," he said, his voice nearly a shout. Even a deaf person would have been able to hear the panic in his tone. "Are you working with him? Is that why you're not listening? Did he recruit you?"

The question hung awkwardly in the air, revealing something uncomfortable to Leo about the situation. He was caught between two opposing forces and being asked to choose a side based on ignorant trust. There was no world in which he made a good decision here.

Leo took one more deliberate step forward, taking him past the barrel of the gun and into safety. The gunman turned his head and seemed to consider the situation. His hand dropped down towards his belt, where Leo assumed he kept a knife or a sidearm. Leo shot his hand towards the man's wrist in reaction, hoping he might be able to stop him from arming himself.

Surely he, a journalist, wouldn't be able to stop the skilled soldier. He had no training, no idea what he was doing. His actions, right though they might have been in intent, were foolish and had led to certain death.

But when the soldier grunted with confusion and Leo saw that he held the man's arm in his hand, he was less convinced. Perhaps the training that the soldier had gone through hadn't been very difficult. He certainly wasn't very strong, nor did he seem to have any idea how to break Leo's grip on him.

A smile began to grow on Leo's face as he squeezed, curious to see if he could hurt the rifleman. His bones creaked under the pressure and he groaned in pain. Even still, Leo found that he wasn't using anywhere near all of his strength.

Out of curiosity, he squeezed as hard as he could, just to see what happened. He expected another pained groan, but what followed horrified him beyond anything he would have imagined. The man's forearm shattered completely, leaving his hand dangling by a few ligaments and tendons from the remnants of his once-whole arm. The man screamed in pain and Leo reeled back with confusion.

His head pounded.

He blinked and saw a hatchet driven through the man's arm instead. He blinked again and the bone had been shattered by his grip. The scars on Leo's chest burned. This wasn't supposed to have happened.

This wasn't the way that it had happened.

It took a while before Leo could remember anything again.

| |

Leo woke up once again, irritated by how often he seemed to be doing that. Hank was nowhere to be seen and it was bright outside. He was near the fire once more, and imagined that Hank had carried him there before doing whatever it was that he did during the day.

A loud thump came from nearby. Leo rose to his feet and went to the window to find Hank chopping wood. Leo chuckled quietly to himself. Dressed in his flannel and with his thick beard, he really did look like a lumberjack.

A jolt of pain shot through Leo's head as he remembered the intruders. Had Hank killed them? And what had happened to the last one? Three conflicting visions kept appearing in his head and he couldn't make sense of them.

Maybe a day of labor would ease his mind. He found an extra pair of work boots by the front door, imagined Hank wouldn't mind if he wore them, and joined the lumberjack outside.

Hank nodded in his direction when he saw Leo and then drove his axehead into a thick log. It didn't go all the way through, so he pulled it out and swung again, careful to hit it in the same place as last time. Once again, it hadn't been enough. The third strike, however, swung true and the log fell off of the stump in two pieces.

"Do you wanna try?" Hank asked gruffly. From up close, Leo could see the sweat on his brow and the cadence of his breathing. He had been up for a while chopping, it seemed. Which was odd to realize, as the pile of firewood wasn't nearly as big as he would have expected.

"Sure," Leo said as he rose to his feet.

Hank placed a thick log on the chopping stump and then handed Leo the ax. "It's pretty simple, really," he explained. "All you have to do is cut straight down," he said, making a chopping motion with his hand. "If you deviate to the side at all, it isn't going to work as well."

"Why straight down?" Leo asked, feeling a faint cloudiness in his mind. He felt like he should have known the answer to his question but couldn't understand why.

"Just because of the way the tree grows," Hank replied. "It's strong sideways but not so much up-and-down."

Leo shrugged. That was good enough for him, especially so as it was obvious that that was all that Hank knew. Maybe he could come up with a better answer himself, later.

"And I just have to swing the ax into the log?" Leo asked, pausing before doing so. He was nervous. What if he did something wrong? He didn't want Hank to think him dumb, or worse yet, useless.

Hank sighed. "It's really not that complicated. Just take a breath, relax, and drive the axehead deep into wood. I like to imagine that I'm trying to strike the stump beneath the log rather than the log itself."

Leo frowned and did his best to follow Hank's mental direction. Yes, that made more sense to him, too. So with the mind of a man that was attempting to split the stump, Leo drove the ax into the log.

With a powerful explosion, three things happened simultaneously. First, the log exploded into more pieces than Leo could count. Second, the handle of the ax broke in two, the shorter part flying out of Leo's hand while the other stayed attached to the head. And third, the stump split, the gap so wide one might have imagined that it had been born from the breaking of the very tectonic plates.

Wide-eyed and slack-jawed, Hank carefully walked over to where the stump had once been. He stopped at the edge and stared into the fissure, face wild with amazement.

"Did you just?..."

Leo stepped up beside the lumberjack and nodded.

Deep inside the fissure lay the axehead, smoldering against the bedrock. It sat beneath layers of permafrost, mycelium, and stone. And Leo had been able to do that with just a woodcutter's ax.

| | |

After his impressive display of strength earlier that day, Hank refused to leave Leo's side. It was as if he were a religious zealot proving his faith. Everything Leo needed, he tended to. Everything that Leo did, he did as well. It would have been bothersome if Leo weren't quite so lonely.

Leo realized at some point just how hungry he was. When was the last time he had eaten? Most of his time had been spent sleeping, so he doubted that he was at any risk of starvation, but his stomach still urged him to eat.

When he mentioned this to Hank, the man's eyes lit up. "Would stew be fine?" the lumberjack asked.

"As long as it's edible," Leo said with a laugh. It was hard to think about anything other than food at the moment.

Hank ducked out of the cabin, presumably to go hunting or find a stash of food, and returned a couple minutes later. He held a burlap sack over his shoulder. It appeared full, and Leo could only imagine what it held. Pork? Bread? Cheese? Apples and berries? His mouth watered as his imagination wandered.

Hank dropped the sack near the fire, then went and retrieved a pot. It was larger than any pot Leo had ever seen, probably even big enough to fit a grown man. Hank placed it over the fire, hanging by three chains, and then went outside again. When he came back, he had a shovelful of snow, which he promptly dumped into the pot.

"This'll go a bit faster if you help," Hank said idly.

Leo grabbed the other shovel and helped his friend. His friend. How long had it been since he had called someone that?

A memory flashed through his mind, this time of an unfamiliar woman and a child. They stood in a bright white house, laughing and smiling.

Had they been his friends?

When they were done shoveling, Hank tended to the fire to make sure it was strong enough to get the water to a boil. From what he claimed, soup was incredibly easy to make once you had boiling water. After that, according to Hank, you kind of just dumped everything in and hoped it tasted right.

But what he did after didn't look nearly as easy as Hank claimed. For the next half hour, Hank was a tornado of mixing, tasting, stirring, and mixing again. Every time that Leo thought his friend was done, he would change something and the soup would require more attention.

Just when Leo had lost hope that he would be able to eat soon, Hank announced that the soup was done. Leo breathed a sigh of relief. It smelled incredible. Salts and fats wafted through the air, taunting Leo with the nutrients that he needed.

Hank handed him a bowl and served him as much soup as it could carry.

"I'll go grab you a spoon-" Hank started, and then began to laugh as he saw Leo slurping ravenously from his bowl.

It burned his tongue as it went down, but Leo didn't care. It tasted too good for him to stop. It only took a moment for him to finish. He thrust his cleaned bowl to Hank. "More, please."

Hank served him again, and once again, Leo drank it all down in less than a minute.

"You like it?" Hank asked with a smile. Something about the way he looked at Leo was strange, almost creepy. That was odd.

"I don't even know what it tastes like," Leo replied. "I just know that I need to eat."

Before serving Leo a third bowl, Hank went and got him a spoon. For some reason, Leo had been expecting it to be silver, but like most things in Hank's house, it had been carved from wood.

"This time, take your time and savor each bite. I want to know if you like this recipe so I can make it again."

Restraining himself, Leo obliged. The meat was well-cooked and tender. From the taste of it, it was pork, though something felt a bit off about it. Other than that he could now clearly taste the beans and potatoes, which too had been cooked to perfection. All in all, Leo was impressed and grateful to have Hank as a companion. A lumberjack that could cook was just about the best thing that he could have stumbled upon.

Filled with food and gratitude, Leo ate until he couldn't anymore, and then he fell asleep, feeling better than he could ever remember.

|

The door was still broken. It lay shattered in and about the cabin, a reminder of the attack that they had experienced the night before. Hank had wanted to fix it immediately in the morning, but

Leo had been less than capable of helping before eating. After the soup and a good hour to digest it, though, Leo was more than happy to do his best to help the lumberjack repair the cabin.

When they got outside, Hank explained the repair process. It was quite a bit more complicated than Leo had been expecting, and he stopped listening about halfway through the explanation. If something was truly important, Hank could explain it again.

Hank handed him an ax, one that wasn't broken it seemed, and told Leo to go chop down a few thick trees. Those were his exact words. "A few thick trees." Leo cursed as he wandered into the woods with the ax. What did that mean? Did they all have to be the same type of wood? How thick did he mean? Maybe he was overthinking it a bit, but he didn't want to do a bunch of work and have to do it all again because of a misunderstanding.

He went to the thickest tree he could find and began to chop. He knew from before, with the stump, that the ax wasn't going to be strong enough to handle all of his strength, so he swung carefully, testing its limits.

The first hit stuck with a thud, shaking the trunk of the tree. It had only gone in about a quarter of the way. He ripped it free of the trunk and struck again, this time with more force. It got a bit over halfway through. Leo realized at this point that he didn't know how to properly use an ax. Not that that was going to stop him. He swung once more, with just a bit more force than the last hit, and this time went almost all the way through. He ripped the ax free and prepared to strike once again when he heard the wood began to creak.

He took a step back as the tree toppled and fell to the ground with a crash, the wood groaning from the impact. Leo walked to the top of the tree, grabbed a branch, then dragged it back to camp. He had hoped that Hank would be there to approve or disapprove of his work, but he was nowhere to be found. Deciding that he should stop worrying, Leo did his best to swallow his anxiety and went back into the woods to continue working. He did this a few more times until he had brought the five thickest trees he could find.

Once he was done, Leo sat on a stump and waited for Hank to return. The sun eased its way across the sky, and he began to grow worried. What if something had happened to Hank? What if he had fallen and hurt himself?

It would be best to go look for him, Leo figured. He would have appreciated the same sort of consideration from Hank.

So on his way he went, looking for his one and only friend. Almost immediately, he noticed that there were footprints in the snow leading around the cabin. Leo followed them, careful not to obscure them with his own.

He came upon a single, smooth mound of snow, which was near two similar piles that had been disturbed. Leo went to the smooth one and examined it. It was long and thin, and no more than a foot and a half high.

Well, that was strange. The more Leo thought about it, the more the mound seemed to resemble the shape of a body. He dug into the snow, and not even an inch lower did he make contact with something smooth and dark. He brushed the snow off a bit more, and realized that it was body armor.

The exact same body armor that the intruders had worn the day before.

Hank had buried the men outside of the cabin. For a moment, Leo appreciated the respect his friend had shown their enemies. They deserved a proper burial, even if they had attacked him and Hank.

But something wasn't right. Not exactly. It made sense not to bury the bodies below the snow considering the season. The ground was thick with permafrost and a hole deep enough to hold a body would be incredibly difficult to dig.

What bothered Leo were the two disturbed piles of snow. He didn't need to dig through them to realize that Hank had moved the bodies. Why had he done that? Where had he taken them?

Even worse than that, Hank hadn't told him about the bodies in the first place, and he had already ruined the smooth layer of snow over the last one near the cabin. Regardless of how well he tried to cover his tracks, Hank would discover what he had done.

Something within Leo itched, urging him to keep searching. It was an unparalleled curiosity, a feeling that was foreign and familiar at the same time.

Like a ravenous dog, he ripped through the snow, uncovering the body. When he was done, he stepped back to see the corpse in full. The first thing he noticed was the frost and blood that thinly covered the fallen rifleman. This wasn't a surprise. What was interesting, though, was where the blood was.

From his arm, Leo could see that this was the man whose arm he had crushed. Even so, the majority of the redness was coming from his legs. Leo knelt down and took a closer look, poking at the body with a stick.

His clothes had been cut methodically, in a way that didn't seem to align with how the attack had gone. Obviously Hank had been the one to do it, and now Leo wanted to know why.

The closer he got, the more obvious it was that the cuts had been made to remove flesh from his lower legs and thighs. They had been used to remove meat. Leo felt himself gag and turned away.

Taking heavy breaths, he did a lap around the cabin to collect his thoughts. They were in the middle of the wilderness. It made sense to want to use all of their resources. More than likely, Hank was using the meat to trap and get food, like bears and wolves.

Or maybe he wanted the bodies to not get eaten, so he removed the meat so they could be respected in death. Leo set his jaw and nodded. That had to be it. Hank was a good man, and he wouldn't want even his enemies to have the disrespect of getting eaten.

Even with this theory in mind, Leo knew that he wasn't fully convinced. He needed more information, more evidence, before he was going to be willing to accept anything. He arrived back at the three mounds and did his best to cover the last of the bodies with snow. The other two mounds had tracks away from them from where Hank had dragged them across the ground.

Leo took one more look at the cabin. He didn't have to follow. He could stay and enjoy the fire until Hank got back, living in ignorant bliss all the while. But he knew that he couldn't. It didn't sit right with him. If he was to believe that his friend was a good man, then he would need to prove it, and to do that, he would have to wander into the shadows of the forest.

| |

Leo hid behind a tree and watched Hank kick one of the bodies off the edge of a cliff. There was a moment of silence and then a wet thud. Hank spit into the air and then turned and headed back to the cabin.

For a moment, Hank seemed to be intently staring at Leo's hiding spot, but then he turned and continued on his way. Leo breathed a sigh of relief and waited a few minutes before following his friend.

What would he tell Hank when he got back? Would he need an excuse to explain why he had left? Leo considered this for a moment. A prepared story wouldn't hurt, and if Hank got suspicious about anything, it would be good to have one ready.

He tried his best to think of something that made sense, but had trouble focusing. He couldn't get the image of Hank kicking the dead rifleman off the cliff out of his head.

Another image flashed through his head of Hank screaming. Leo blinked. That had never happened. But he felt so certain that it had. That it was what was supposed to have happened, if such a feeling could be described.

His chest ached and he became sharply aware of the two scars that marked it.

The image faded to be replaced by one of Hank sharpening a machete, only to turn around once he had noticed that Leo was watching. This, too, felt as if it were what had truly happened, though Leo couldn't understand why.

What was going on?

Suddenly it didn't feel quite so safe to follow Hank back to the cabin. The other man was dangerous. Everything he had seen had shown that the lumberjack was dangerous and volatile.

Dangerous and volatile. Dangerous and volatile. The words rang through his mind with deep importance, and Leo couldn't remember why. Who, or what, was dangerous and volatile?

Trusting his instincts, Leo decided that it would be best to return to the cabin since he was feeling unsafe. Hank would know what to do. His friend always knew exactly how to help.

Leo shook his head to clear away his confusion and headed back home. Home. How long had it been since he had used that word? Maybe his fate would lead him to the answers. It had brought him this far, to the safety of Hank's cabin, but where it would take him next, he had no idea.

Maybe Hank had been his destination. Maybe this was his final utopia.

| | |

Moonlight shone through the window as Hank and Leo prepared for bed. Leo's mouth was beginning to feel as though it desperately needed a cleaning, and his hair was getting thick with grease, though he wasn't sure how he was supposed to combat these problems. Hank didn't seem too bothered, so Leo resolved to remain stoic and ignore his internal complaints.

They hadn't spoken much since coming back from rebuilding the door, which stood even stronger than the first door, and Leo was trying his best to change that. If he were to call Hank his friend, they would need to talk. Plus, the other man was the closest person he could find to give him the answers he desired regarding the end of the world and its current state.

Much to Leo's surprise, Hank was the first to break their shared silence.

"Where are you from?" the lumberjack asked as they were laying down their skins on the wooden floor. They were the closest things to beds that they had in the cabin.

Leo scratched his chin and looked up at his friend. "I'm not sure. I remember a city, but other than that my mind is a little foggy."

Hank nodded as if that made sense. "It affected us all differently, didn't it."

"The end?" Leo clarified.

"Yeah," Hank replied. "It took me a while to piece things together myself, and a lot of it came from other people that I've met since."

Leo chewed on his lip as he tried to figure out how to steer the conversation to giving him the answers he sought. "Where were you when it started?" he asked.

Hank sat back with a look of nostalgia on his face. "I was on a camping trip with some friends," he answered. "Rob and Brad. Good guys. We served together and then never quite figured out how not to be together."

"You were in the military?"

"The marines. We met when we were still kids." Hank blinked as if he had made a mistake and then his face hardened. "What about you? Where were you?"

"I can't remember," Leo said honestly. "I think I was at home. Maybe I wasn't. I can only picture that city, the one I think I lived in, collapsing into a pile of dust. If anyone was there at the time, they probably died."

Hank snorted. "They definitely died. There's hardly anyone left on this blue ball."

Leo didn't like how easily his friend said that. How comfortable he was with the idea of death.

"Are Rob and Brad still around?" Leo asked.

Hank shook his head slightly. "Not anymore."

Leo waited to see if he would elaborate, but he didn't.

"What happened to them?"

Hank frowned and tilted his head. "I'm guessing the same thing that happened to that precious city of yours," he said.

A lock built of silence fell upon their conversation. Its combination was complex, and Leo didn't know whether or not he could crack it. Perhaps he could change the subject? No, he didn't want to. He wanted to hear about the end of the world, to know its truth inside and out. Maybe he could redirect the conversation away from Hank's friends? They seemed to really bother him.

"If you could have one wish, what would it be?" Leo asked eventually. It felt like the perfect question. The open-endedness meant that he would learn a lot about his friend regardless of his answer, and considering the direction of their conversation, it was likely that his answer was going to be related to the end of the world. Leo stifled a proud smile and waited for the lumberjack to respond.

"That's a good question," Hank said after a moment. "Not one that I've considered a lot. The world isn't quite so forgiving to grant wishes to men like me." He said nothing for a moment and then continued. "I'd probably wish for the capacity to survive."

"To survive?" Leo asked, confused. That's not what he had been expecting.

"To survive. No matter what"

|

Leo couldn't sleep. He stared at the ceiling and traced his eyes over the grain of the wood. It was mesmerizing. How did trees grow to give the boards such intricate patterns? For that matter, how did trees grow in general? The more he learned, the more he came to understand just how little he knew.

Hank snored softly across the room. His breath was one of the factors contributing to Leo's insomnia, but it wasn't that alone. His mind kept going back to their conversation, specifically, to what he had said.

He hadn't been able to remember much about his life until they had started talking. Now, though, the details poured back into his conscious memory as if whatever blockage that had been there before had broken.

Not only had Leo been a journalist, but he had had a family. A child and a wife. He couldn't remember their names or what they looked like. He could only recall how they made him feel. His wife had been so warm, so supportive, and his child was the source of more of his happiness than anyone else.

Why didn't he know more.

Leo clenched his jaw and tried to focus harder. What were their names? What were some of the things that he and his family had done together? Where were they now?

While he didn't know the answers to these questions, he tried to imagine what they might be all the same. The only things he dared not assume were their names, as they felt too sacred to face the burden of his mind.

So he closed his eyes and imagined what he might look like being a family-man.

They liked to go on hikes together, with picnics at the end. Their child always complained about her feet hurting, but Leo knew that she only did it to get more attention from his wife. He could vaguely sense that their child had also been a girl, and that she had been creative and adventurous. She could always make him laugh, and even though she showed that she hated their hikes, she always bragged to her friends about how cool he was for taking her on them. His wife was incredibly loving and did all that she could to support them.

He was having a hard time picturing what his wife might have been like, so Leo focused more on their child so as to avoid the disappointment of a dull imagination.

Hank stirred, breaking Leo's concentration. Suddenly, with a burning sensation in Leo's chest, the world split in two. In one world, Hank got up and approached Leo, while in the other, he went back to sleep. In one, he told Leo to get up and follow him, and in the other, he tossed a bit beneath his blankets. In one, he led Leo into the woods in the dead of night, and in the other, he huddled on his animal skin.

But both had one thing in common. Leo could practically taste the fear emanating from his friend.

| |

When the morning came, the calm that so often arrived with

waking, was absent. Leo stretched to feel his body, and it replied with tension. Pain arced through his neck and back and his teeth ached dully from grinding.

He couldn't get the images of Hank out of his mind.

No amount of framing or reframing helped him understand his friend. Why was he afraid? What was bothering him so much that he was either going to leave him in the woods, or save himself by avoiding the issue?

More importantly, how was Leo remembering the present?

That's the best way he could describe it. When his perception of the world broke, it didn't feel as though he was receiving a vision from some divine entity; instead it felt the same as a memory that just so happened to run concurrently with reality.

Even his internal explanation was confusing. It didn't make sense that that could be the case. One of those two things had to have happened, and one of them had. Hank hadn't led him into the woods. He had stayed in bed.

Why then, did Leo have such a strong sense that he had done both?

The question wasn't going to go away, and no amount of thinking about it was helping, so Leo got out of bed, put on the boots that Hank had lent him, and went to chop wood to distract his cluttered mind.

Strangely, though, the ax that he usually used was nowhere to be found. He looked around for a while, checking all of the places that he might have left it, but it never turned up.

As more time passed, paranoia creeped into his mind like an infection. He had never lost the ax before. There were only so many places it could be. It was a goddamn ax, it wasn't something that was easily lost.

Everything kept pointing to the same thing. No matter how he tried to look at it, Leo continued to come to the same conclusion.

Hank had taken the ax.

Which, by itself, was fine. It was Hank's ax, and if he was using it, then Leo wasn't going to complain. The problem was that Hank wasn't using it. He had taken a machete and some rope and gone trapping.

He hadn't taken the ax with him.

Which meant that he hadn't just taken the ax; he had also taken the ax from Leo. He had hidden it for a reason.

Why?

Did he not trust Leo?

Why?

Did it have anything to do with his memories of the present?

How?

Hank couldn't have known about those. So then what was it? What had changed? Leo's mind spiraled as he tried to imagine what could be creating distance between him and his friend. So much had changed since the night before.

As to why, that was still a mystery. So many things were. His mind, which he wanted to rely on like the keystone of an arch, was crumbling and failing before his eyes. The gaps in his knowledge obvious, Leo went and stared at the fire while waiting for his only friend to return. He hoped that would be soon. He hated being alone.

-

Blood trickled down Leo's cheek. He was covered in cuts and bruises, and his neck ached. He vaguely remembered a fight with Hank after an argument, but his head was swimming and it was hard to collect his thoughts.

Something had gone wrong. Something had gone horribly wrong, and now he was going to pay. Leo didn't understand. All he had done was talk to his friend about the riflemen, the intruders, and what he had with their bodies. Leo had watched him kick them into the cavern, covered in blood, and wanted to know why.

His innate curiosity had begged him to ask. His instincts screamed at him not to, telling him that he was making a mistake, and he asked anyway.

Such was the life of a journalist.

All in all, Leo was happy to have lived the life that he had. His wife and daughter had been proud to call him Husband and Father, and now he was going to join them. He just wished he could remember them better.

Images of his daughter, her smile mischievous yet knowing, floated into his mind. Her face faded a bit more every time he tried to picture her. His wife, her name a whisper in the wind, was passing along with their child. It felt as though the beating Hank had given him had beaten them further out of his mind.

It took him a moment to realize that he was coming to terms with his death. This was the end. But maybe that was okay. Maybe he had come far enough, lived a good enough life, that he didn't need to fight to change what Hank was doing to him.

Maybe.

As much as he tried to succumb to his wounds, to go limp and let Hank drag him through the forest to the cliff that would be his doom, he couldn't convince himself that it was the right path to follow. It would certainly be easiest, and maybe he could see his wife and daughter sooner if he believed in something like that.

But just because it was the easiest, didn't mean that it was the best. Leo blinked and breathed clairty into his mind. This wasn't a good death. This was brutality. This was murder. Hank might think that he deserved to die like this, but Leo knew better.

He took a few moments to gather some energy and then began to scramble, trying to break Hank's grip and get away. Something hard struck Leo in the head, and his world went black.

-

Wind howled through the canyon, waking Leo from his concussed stupor. He tried to yawn and stretch the stiffness out of his arms, but they wouldn't move. He didn't need to look to know that they had been tied above his head. His feet, on the other hand, had not been given such a treatment. They dangled freely against the walls of the rocky cavern.

So he had failed to free himself then. He tugged on the ropes that bound his wrists, but was too hurt to properly move. This would be his demise. This was the last of Leo, whoever he was.

Not knowing what else to do, he listened to the wind. At first, it was just deafening, its force being multiplied by the funnel of the canyon. The more Leo listened, however, the more it almost sounded like it carried a deeper sort of meaning.

It was almost as if it were speaking to him. He strained to hear the wind, trying to make sense of the white noise.

"How's it hanging?" the wind asked.

Leo frowned. The wind had said that to him? He looked around and flinched when he saw a man seating on the top of the cliff, kicking his feet idly. He had a nonchalant posture and white hair that flew in the wind like snow. There was something else odd about the way he looked, but Leo couldn't quite place it.

"Who are you?" Leo asked through gritted teeth. His wrists burned from the rope. The knots were tightening with every movement of his body.

The man laughed. "I open with 'How's it hanging,' and that's how you respond? No clever response? Nothing?" He pouted with mock disappointment. "I was expecting better."

"I'm a little tied up at the moment," Leo replied as he nodded up to where his hands were bound above his head.

With a laugh and a clap, the man's face lit up. Subtly, his idle kicking became more enthusiastic. "That's more like it," the man said. "My name is Tim."

"I'm-"

Tim waved dismissively. "Yes, yes. I know." His expression was suddenly much more serious. "You need my help."

Leo glanced up at his hands and then back at Tim. "It certainly would be appreciated."

"Yes, I think it would," Tim said with a distant look in his eyes. "Nobody wants to die."

Leo frowned when it was obvious that he wasn't going to continue. "So, are you going to help me?" A frosty breeze blew through his cloak, sending a chill down his spine. "I'm starting to get really cold."

Tim looked sharply at Leo, and suddenly he could tell what was so off-putting about the newcomer. His eyes were completely white.

"You are a plaything for the gods," Tim said.

"I don't think so-"

Tim shook his head. "I am not going to argue this point with you. This is what you are." He paused and seemed to consider his words. "But you don't have to be."

"How do you mean?" Leo asked. He wasn't following the conversation in the least.

Tim sighed. "You used to have a life. I know you know it. I can see it in your Identity, but one doesn't need to look so deep. You ooze the loneliness that can only come from a man that has lost his utopia."

Leo clenched his jaw and looked down.

"Don't you ever wonder what happened? How you could have lost so much? Why you don't remember anything?"

"Of course, I wonder," Leo snapped. "I can't get them out of my head."

"You don't need to let them control you anymore," Tim said almost too quietly for Leo to hear. "You can break free before they break you."

"How?"

Once again, Tim sighed. "I could help you, you know. I really could. I could wave my hand and free you from your bonds. I could give you warmth and a life that you might one day learn to enjoy. But I could never give you the one thing that you truly need."

"And what's that?" Leo asked as dread began to settle upon him. He wasn't going to get any help, was he.

"Closure."

They didn't speak for a few minutes, and Leo's slight chills turned into an uncontrollable shiver.

"You're unlucky that I was the one to come," Tim laughed, his voice starting to sound a bit muffled. Leo was having a hard time staying awake. He hadn't realized how tired he was until the other man had spoken. "My brother is better when it comes to Fate."

"I'm unlucky in general," Leo grumbled.

"Yes, you are," Tim agreed. "More than most, I'm afraid. Well, that is unless you choose not to follow the path that you're on."

"You called me a plaything for the gods," Leo said, "and you say that I can choose not to be. How?"

Tim's face fell as he pointed below Leo. "I'm sorry, my child. I wish there were another way."

It took Leo a moment to understand what the other man was saying. The cavern was so deep that he couldn't see the bottom. Did he want to fall and join the other men that Hank had killed? Did he want to give the lumberjack the satisfaction of winning?

He turned back to say something else to Tim, anything else, but nobody was there. A lump formed in Leo's throat. He looked up and noticed that there was a knife in his left hand. Tim must have given it to him.

Suddenly the drop seemed endless. His stomach lurched as he imagined what it would feel like to fall. The knife was heavy in his hand. Did he have the strength to do it?

No. It wasn't about strength. It was about trust. Did he trust that Tim was telling him the truth, or not? Did he value the word of a stranger enough to let it control his life. And why did letting one random person control him mean that he was setting himself free?

It didn't make sense. He had no reason to listen to Tim. But now he did have something that he didn't before. Maybe the knife could help him escape.

Leo looked up and examined the knots around his wrists. The rope which bound him was hanging on an iron rod that stuck out from the cliff. This meant that if either side of the rope were to break, the other would lose tension and he would immediately fall.

He moved one hand up and pulled the other down to test the friction of the rope against the rod. It moved easier than he would have liked. It almost felt as though the rod or rope had been oiled, though Leo couldn't be sure that that was the case.

It was difficult for him to see any possible methods for escape. No matter what he decided to do, it seemed as though he would fall to his death. Leo racked his brain and began to look around to see if there was anything nearby that he might be able to use to help himself.

Not too far away, a large piece of rock jutted out of the cliff wall. It almost looked like it would be the perfect hand hold. Maybe if he could swing, Leo would be able to grab it.

Even if he couldn't, though, the idea of climbing had cemented itself into his weakening mind. If the wall was climbable, then he wasn't in such a bad place as he would have otherwise thought.

Leo realized then that no matter how he went about getting to the top, there was a clear order of operations that he needed to tend to. The first thing he needed to do was make his hand useful. This would either come by freeing his hands from the rope, or by doing something to ascend over the iron rod to release the tension. The second step would be to make his way up the cliff, given that he hadn't done that to release his hands. It wasn't a complicated set of operations, but it was certainly going to be challenging to accomplish both.

However, now that he had framed the problem in such a simple way, Leo didn't feel quite so daunted by it. It wasn't going to be that hard to get free. He just had to use his hands and then climb. Use his hands and then climb. Use his hands and then climb. The words rung through his head.

But how was he going to do that?

Reframing the problem in his head didn't magically make himself not tied up, and it didn't remove the shiver that was distracting him so much from the task at hand.

All of a sudden, he was struck by the humor of his situation. He had been dragged through the forest by his only friend only to be tied up, not killed, so that he could talk to a strange-looking man who wanted Leo to kill himself.

Leo first started to chuckle, then laugh, and then cackle. He did so until his lungs burned and his stomach hurt, and even then he did it a bit more. It felt good to laugh. The more he did it, the more the shiver faded and the better he felt.

Tim had been confident but still incorrect. Leo wasn't unlucky. No, he wasn't unlucky at all. In fact, he was quite a bit luckier than he had any right being. After everything he had been through, it didn't make sense to him that he was still alive.

The world had supposedly ended, and there he still stood.

He had trudged through icy forest, on the brink of hypothermia, and there he still stood.

He had caught a murderer dealing with his victims, and instead of joining them, there Leo still stood.

It didn't take a genius to see that something, or someone, had blessed him. It had given him the tools and instincts to survive when he had no right to. Maybe that's why he was still alive and his family wasn't. Well, never mind that.

A small, icy cliff wasn't going to mark his change of luck. Not while he still had feeling in his fingers and a beating heart in his body.

Slowly at first, Leo began trying to turn himself around. All he needed to do was to get his side caught on the wall, and then he figured he could completely spin himself. He did this by generating rotation in his hips and swinging his body around it.

When it became clear that this slower approach wasn't going to work, Leo became more violent with his rotational movement, which from the outside appeared to be violent jerking. The rocky cliff scraped against his back, tearing his clothes and skin, but he persevered nonetheless. Nothing was going to stop him from surviving, not even the harsh winter or whatever other unfortunate circumstances he found himself in.

And then it happened. Leo's side made contact with the wall and his body teetered on the brink of all that he had accomplished over the course of the past few minutes. One shift back and all would be lost, and with one slight push forward he would be saved.

A puff of wind blew through the canyon, as if given to him

by some gracious divinity, sending Leo over the edge and towards the cliff, front-facing. He kissed the stone with glee. Now, all he had to do was climb up and all would be well.

Leo started out by pulling up on the rope with his hands and climbing the wall with his feet. There was a twist in the rope that added to the tension, and in any other situation this might have been a problem. However, at the present, the extra tension served to tighten the rope and lift his hands just a smidge higher than they had been prior to the twist, allowing him to climb higher without searching the rock for handholds.

As his feet got higher, even the twist couldn't keep the required tension to make the climb feasible, so Leo shimmied his hands up the rope until they reached the iron rod from which Hank had hung him. He moved his feet up a bit higher, and then paused as he was about to unwrap the rope from the rod. Were he to fall, this was his lifeline. It was true that it was a sort of prison for him, and freeing himself might feel like the obvious right answer, but he needed to consider his options before committing to that.

And then he was struck by a cold wind, and all semblance of clear and careful thought went out like a candle in a gale. He needed to climb and couldn't do that with the rope. He had almost forgotten about the knife in his hand after losing so much heat, blood, and ultimately feeling. Leo sawed at the rope until it broke, then clumsily brought the knife between his teeth as he finished the last few feet of his climb.

Just a few more feet, and he would be over the edge.

Just a few more steps, and his life wouldn't be in someone else's hands.

Just a few more inches, and he could finally be free of the curse of Hank and whatever gods might be controlling him, if any were.

Leo clawed at the frozen dirt at the top of the ledge and pulled himself onto the ground atop the cliff. His fingers ached and stung from the sharp stone wall. Panting, he collapsed into the snow and stared into the sky.

His chest ached at first and then began to shake.

Llooped

It took him a moment to realize why. At first he had thought that it was from exhaustion. His body had used a ton of energy and adrenaline to accomplish that ascent.

And then he had imagined that it was from the cold. Were he to go much longer without a decent fire, his body would begin to fail and he would die of hypothermia.

But then, in the cold of winter, in a place more desolate than many can understand, Leo came to understand what the shaking was.

Laughter.

| |

Hank came back from his hunt covered in blood. He barged in the front door with a wild look in his eyes and a stench that burned Leo's lungs. It was the smell of death. Just being in the presence of him made Leo wanted to crawl away and hide, but Hank was his friend and was bringing food, so he ignored his instincts and went to help.

"The hunt went poorly?" Leo asked, motioning to the blood. It looked like the lumberjack was going to need quite a lot of medical attention due to his wounds. It was difficult to lose as much blood as he had and still be standing.

Hank frowned. "It actually went quite well," he said. "There was just a bit of a fight. That's all."

Something about what Hank had just said tickled Leo's mind. "A fight?" he asked. "With what?"

Hank tilted his head and then revealed a toothy grin. "My prey. But never mind that. Help me prepare the stew."

Leo started towards the lumberjack and then paused. Deep down, he could feel that something was off. His mind flashed to images of intruders wielding rifles. Right. He had forgotten about them. Where were they now? What had happened to them?

And most importantly, why was he thinking of them now?

"Have you ever killed someone?" Leo probed. His subconscious was trying to tell him something.

Hank raised an eyebrow. "Of course, I have. You saw me do it. It was in self-defense, remember?"

Leo stumbled back. Everything was starting to make sense. Memories forgotten were coming to the forefront of his mind. He could see more clearly now. The riflemen had been hidden in snowbanks outside of the cabin. They had been carved bloody.

And now he understood why.

"It was in self-defense?" Leo asked, slowly retreating from Hank. "Why did they break into the cabin?"

Hank laughed tensely. "They're raiders. They probably wanted food." He paused. "No, wait! It's possible that they didn't have a place to stay and wanted to live in my cabin." His face fell flat and he stared seriously at Leo. "Don't you think that's most likely?"

Leo shook his head. "No, that doesn't make any sense." He was suddenly able to remember the conversation he had had with the third and final rifleman. "You're dangerous. That's what they told me. And they knew you. I think they came here to kill you."

Hank furrowed his brow. "It's not possible to stay alive in this environment without being dangerous. That's why I've kept you. You're a weapon, in need of sharpening sure, but a weapon all the same. Dangerous men survive. They were just afraid of me."

Leo chewed on his cheek as he tried to organize his racing thoughts. Pieces of a puzzle were falling neatly into place in front of him. "Where are all of the animals?" he asked.

The lumberjack appeared confused. "The animals?"

Leo nodded. "The squirrels, the bears, the birds. Where are they? I haven't seen any during my time here. Have you?"

"Not many animals survived the end of the world," Hank replied. "I catch what I can and we eat them, but it's difficult when there are so few."

"No, you don't. Stop lying to me." Leo could feel the heat rising in his face. "I already know. You don't need to lie to me anymore."

Hank opened his mouth to speak, but Leo continued.

"There are no tracks in the snow, no sounds of nature. This forest is completely dead. But somehow you aren't. Somehow, you can make meat out of thin air."

The lumberjack's face hardened. "I did what I had to do to survive."

"No you didn't!" Leo shrieked, his voice shaky. It was so loud that the cabin shook and snow fell from the roof with a dull thud. "You didn't have to do that. You didn't have to eat them. You didn't have to make me eat them."

At first Hank said nothing. He stared at Leo blankly and then the corner of his mouth turned upwards. "You're smarter than I thought, I'll give you that. How did you figure it out?"

Leo threw up in his mouth. The lumberjack had no defense. If anything, he was amused.

How could Hank have done something like that?

Yet as much as Leo wished he could throw all of his blame and hate at the lumberjack for making him a cannibal, he knew that he couldn't. Leo should have known better. He should have figured it out before eating the stew. It was so obvious. There were no animals. It was so obvious.

But he had been so hungry.

No, that wasn't a justification. There was no reconciliation that could dampen this pain, that could alter this part of his identity. He was a cannibal, regardless of whether or not his former friend had made him that way.

So, with nothing else to do, and nowhere to go, he ran away from Hank, he ran away from his past, and he ran away from his mistakes and his pain.

"Solitude"

Midday

Leo remembered being surprised to find a settlement not too far from Hank's cabin. They called themselves a township, but even that felt too grand a word for the small collection of huts huddled within the feeble walls that they trusted to protect them.

The village was known as Dagsland, and it was a happy, but serious place.

He vaguely remembered stumbling into the collection of homes, delirious from hunger and hypothermia, only to be accepted with open arms by the settlers. They were kind for that.

Though it was hard to forget that Hank had been the same way at first.

Leo tried not to focus too much on his cannibalistic lumberjack friend and instead on where his life had taken him, but he couldn't do it. In every shadow, he saw bodies. Every pool of water was blood.

He carried an everpresent nausea that nothing could seem to shake.

His only solace was that Dagsland was entirely vegetarian in diet. When he had initially inquired as to why, the Captain had explained that after the end of the world, most of the animals had died after many of the ecosystems had collapsed.

Leo smiled as he thought about that conversation. So he had been right about that after all.

Well, anyways, that meant that he was getting a diet that was a bit more diverse than what he had seen with Hank, and though it was definitely lacking in protein, he wasn't bothered by it. It didn't seem like his muscles needed that much help to be of use.

Presently, he sat near a campfire with a couple of the other villagers. A pot of stew was cooking on top of it, the smell wafting through the air. Leo's stomach ached with hunger.

"What's in it today, Drum?" one of the villagers called. Leo had learned her name at some point, and then immediately forgotten it. He doubted he would ever have a good grasp on their names, in all honesty.

Part of that had to do with how they called each other. Drum wasn't anyone's first name. He was the cook, James Drummond, and since most of the villagers referred to each other by their last names, they had shortened his to make it easier to say.

To Leo, though, their names were a bit too foreign for them to stick in his brain. He just hoped that they wouldn't be too bothered by his poor memory and take it personally.

"Potatoes, carrots, peas, and a bit of chicken broth that I found somewhere," Drum said with a wink. "Don't tell the Captain."

People grinned with anticipation and Leo could understand why. Drum was an immaculate cook even without proper ingredients, so they were all eager to see what he could do when he had more than the bare essentials.

A few minutes later, the stew was ready and they took turns serving themselves. After each person took their share of food, Drum would make a quip that was unique to the person that he was talking to.

For example, when it was a large man's turn to take his food, Drum scoffed and asked him if he should really be eating that much. Leo thought that the comment had been rude, but it was followed by laughter, so perhaps he was wrong.

That was how the serving line was. It was full of jokes, light-hearted insults, and good times. Leo loved watching and was happy to finally be a part of it.

When it was his turn to get food, he spooned the stew into his bowl until he had enough, and then waited expectantly for Drum to say something to him.

But he never did.

The cook just gave him a small smile, and then turned his attention to the villager behind Leo, as if to say 'next.'

Hurt more than he would have liked to admit, Leo sat down and ate his food by himself. No one tried to talk to him. Not that they should have. He wasn't one of them, and he could tell.

X

Other than eating and staring at the campfire, there wasn't much to do in Dagsland. It was clear to Leo that he wasn't alone in this feeling. Outside of meal times, he had only seen the other villagers work out and fight each other. What an interesting experience.

It wouldn't have been so bad if Leo hadn't felt quite so alone. All in all, it wasn't a terrible place to live. He always had food, water, shelter, and a warm fire to come back to.

Of course, he had had all of that before, too. Back when he had lived with Hank. Leo had only been in Dagsland for a couple of days so far, and he had already considered going back to the lumberjack a couple dozen times. Life before the revelation had been good, beautiful even.

With Hank, he had been filled with purpose. They had been a partnership, surviving together. They had chopped wood, made food, built, and slept together. They had been friends.

The thing that bothered Leo most about the situation was not that Hank had lied to him. No, that made sense. Cannibalism wasn't socially acceptable. What bothered him the most was that as a result of his time with the lumberjack, he was beginning to question his notions of good and bad.

This new group, the villagers of Dagsland, would normally be considered good when compared to Hank. After all, they didn't murder and then eat people. But at the same time, they made Leo feel much worse than Hank had. So in that sense, wasn't Hank better than they were? How could the so-called good people treat him so much more poorly than a cannibal?

Bored and irritated, Leo wandered the complex, searching for something to do. As much as he hated the monotony of their life, some of the activities did seem interesting. What was sparring like? And more than anything, he was curious if running in a group was that different than running on your own.

So Leo did the only thing that made sense to him at the time. Armed with his complaints and stresses, he marched through the complex with purpose, towards the only person that had the power to do anything about it.

He was going to speak with the Captain.

Her cabin was away from the city center, near one of the town gates. It was plain, and had he not seen her walk periodically into the building, he wouldn't have known that it was her domicile. There was nothing particularly interesting about it other than an iron plate on the door frame, which none of the other homes had.

Leo approached cautiously, suddenly not feeling the fire of determination that he had felt just a few moments ago. What if she was like the others? What if the Captain just wanted to be left alone, and all he was doing was bothering her?

No, he had to try. He wouldn't get anywhere if he didn't at least try. He took a deep breath and then knocked gently on the iron plate. It bounced against the wood with a clang and then was followed by silence.

A soft wind blew through the town, followed by the sounds of chimes. Leo shuddered and turned around, idly watching Dagsland as he waited. It had only been a few moments since he had knocked, and already they were stretching into an eternity.

Leo turned back and examined the cabin as he waited, resolved not to leave until he had at least spoken to the Captain. Her house, like all of the others, was made of wood. The material was strong, not even showing an ounce of rot. Her house, again, like all of the others, had mud packed between the logs to help keep them together. It was well-packed, showing no signs of flaking.

But then he came back to the iron plate. The one differentiating factor. What did it represent? Why did she display it for everyone to see? Now, with it, she was different. She wasn't one of the people anymore. It was a strong statement, and in Leo's emotional state he was beginning to understand its purpose a little bit more.

Were he in her position, he would have taken it down. He would have done anything to be more like the others, to be collected by their love and be asked to join in on their fun. He never would have pushed himself away.

Leo tapped his foot impatiently as he was reminded of just how long it had been since he had first knocked. "Captain?" he called, rapping his knuckles against the plate once more.

It didn't take long for him to understand that he wasn't wanted. Had she wanted to speak with him, the Captain would have opened the door after the first knock. But he knew that that was a foolish expectation. For he wasn't one of them, and even the Captain wasn't going to tell him otherwise.

Feeling a pit rise in his stomach, Leo turned and walked back towards the cabin that they had given him. It was the only one that hadn't been built the same as the others. They had used a different wood, one with a bit of rot, and an older mud that flaked. It was also the only one, other than the Captain's which wasn't close to the city center.

As he got home, he placed his hand on the doorknob and paused before going inside.

Well, at least his front door didn't have an iron plate.

X

Leo awoke feeling irritated and quickly came to understand that that wasn't going to change anytime soon. This wasn't a fickle sort of irritation. It wasn't the kind you got from a bug in your ear or an itch on your leg. It was the sort of irritation that came from deep dissatisfaction without a means of reconciliation. With nothing else to do, Leo wrapped himself tightly in his coat, and with a scowl, went on a walk around the village.

More than he ever had before, Leo felt trapped. Dagsland was not a town that allowed for freedom or fun. That wasn't the problem, though. The problem was that he had no other options.

The city was to be his home or he was to be homeless.

It was almost as though the gods were laughing at him, making him choose between being a spectre in a peculiar sort of hell or a free spirit in another. What choice did he have? He had to survive, to eat, to sleep properly, and he could get all of those things in Dagsland.

However, this feeling that he was trapped was only a small part of Leo's irritation. He didn't like feeling so dissatisfied. He wished he could look on the township through the eyes of the other villagers to see the home that they saw. They so clearly valued their community, and he wanted to understand why.

On top of that, Leo didn't like that Hank had tricked him so easily. He had seemed so nice at first, offering Leo a place to stay with food to eat. The lumberjack had given him purpose and a life worth living. Leo would have been happy to stay there for a while, he thought.

But most of all, Leo didn't like that he still missed Hank and the friendship that he had offered. They hadn't been the closest of friends, but they had known things about each other. They had shared a routine and a living space. They had recognized that their partnership would benefit each other.

Lost in thought, Leo bumped into someone. "I'm sorry," he said instinctively, turning to see who it was.

"No it's okay," the woman replied. She looked familiar. It was something about the way she carried herself that was distinct from the others. Was it her poise? Her confidence? Leo couldn't quite place his finger on it.

"Did you want something?" she asked.

Leo shook his head after realizing that he had been staring. There was something familiar about the woman. Then it struck him. "Are you the Captain?" he asked.

She smiled. "Yes, I am. I'm sorry, remind me of your name?"

"Leo."

"Around here we often refer to each other by last name," she explained. "Or do you prefer just being called Leo?"

It was in that moment that Leo learned that he didn't know

what his last name was. "Just Leo is fine."

"Well, it's fantastic to be re-introduced to you, Leo," the Captain said with a smile. "I hope you have a good day and enjoy your time in our village." She turned to leave.

"Wait," Leo called out, his voice tantalizingly weak. "I wanted to talk to you about something."

She looked back at him and raised an eyebrow. "What's that?"

Leo's eyes danced over her face as he searched for the words. How was he going to ask her? How did he tell her just how unhappy he was with her town? How was she supposed to even help him? Perhaps talking to her had just been a waste of time.

"Is there something I can do while I'm here?" he offered.

The Captain tilted her head. "And by that you mean?..."

"I want to work. I want to help out. I know how to chop wood and could learn to cook. Really, I just want to do something. Anything."

The Captain seemed to consider what he was saying. "Did nobody come and talk to you about your job yet?"

Leo shook his head. "I hardly know anyone."

"Well that just won't do. No, that won't do at all." She made a show of looking Leo up and down, and while he knew that she was trying to make him feel seen for the first time since arriving to Dagsland, it felt more patronizing than anything.

"I'm stronger than I look," Leo said after an awkward silence had passed between them.

The Captain nodded. "I should hope so. Well, if you'd be interested, we could put you in a squad until you find something that you'd like to do."

Leo shrugged. "What would I do on the squad?"

"Nothing too specialized at the beginning," she admitted. "Mostly, you'd just have a group to train with. There's a bit of sparring, lifting, and running, but I'm sure it's nothing you can't handle."

"That sounds good to me, thank you."

The Captain narrowed her eyes as if she were peering into Leo's soul. It was unsettling. "You seem unsatisfied."

Leo pursed his lips and weighed whether or not he should explain. Was it worth the effort? Just letting the topic go would be easiest, but that wouldn't help him. He needed to talk, and maybe the Captain was the person that needed to listen. He took a deep breath and went on. "In all honesty, I've been a bit frustrated by how little I've been able to help out since arriving. I'm not used to feeling useless."

The Captain furrowed her brow and her gaze softened. "Why didn't you come to me earlier, then? We could always use an extra pair of hands. The dead of winter is not nearly so forgiving to allow us to lounge and enjoy the spoils of our toils." She said this last bit with a light chuckle.

"I did come to you," Leo replied. "Yesterday, I went to your house. You didn't answer."

The Captain's face darkened. "No, I suppose I didn't."

Without another word passing between them, she left him to stand alone in the town center and consider their conversation. The shift had been so sudden, so dramatic, that Leo almost didn't believe that it had happened. Never before had he felt such great relief be replaced by an even greater sense of frustration than he had carried before.

X

If nothing else, Leo was impressed by how efficient the people of Dagsland were. Not even a day after his conversation with the Captain, he had been placed on a squad and was preparing to go on his first run with them.

During this process, Leo learned a few important things about the village. The first was that there was a reason they were so diligent with their training. Back before the end of the world, they had been the police force in a large city, though Leo couldn't remember which one - even though they had told him a few times already.

The second was that many of the buildings in the village were not homes. In fact, most of them weren't. Almost everything close to the town center was used for training or storage, with only a few exceptions.

The third was an extension of the second, but it was still the most important revelation of all three, and it was that other than the Captain, Leo was the only person to have their own house.

For this, his squadmates called him lucky.

What an odd way to say lonely.

They laughed and enjoyed the camaraderie that came with roommates and barracks, while Leo was sequestered to his own quarters every night, his only company his thoughts. Of course, he was no fool. They envied his privacy: he and the Captain were the only ones to truly have it in Dagsland. Perhaps the grass was always greener, and were he to switch places with them he would be just as jealous as they were. He doubted it, though.

They jogged through the town at an easy pace, passing by other squads doing the same. Many of them were in fantastic shape and could run quite fast, but that wasn't true of everyone. They all ran in the same group, so the fastest among the squad had to slow their pace to accommodate the needs of the slowest.

Leo could feel even after their first run that his body wanted to push and go faster. Every step was annoyingly sluggish. Faster. He felt a power in his legs that he had never felt before and only wanted to throw himself forward and sprint. Faster.

They ran for the better part of the morning, and by the end of their workout, everyone, even the fittest in their squad was coated in a thin layer of sweat. Well, everyone except for Leo. His body ached for more exertion, screaming at him to keep going.

Inside their barracks, the squad gathered around a jug of water, which they shared as they dried off with towels. They chatted idly as they drank, and Leo watched from the side. He was observing for a bit with the hopes that he might learn enough about the group to one day be truly accepted.

Their squad was not large, only comprising ten people total, Leo included. So far Leo had only been introduced to the bigger names in their group, those being Ford, Barnes, and Johnson. Like he had learned before, these were their last names, and it was an important part of their culture that they had these special nicknames for each other.

The unfortunate by-product of this was that they had decided he needed a nickname, too, which he had quickly learned couldn't be Leo.

The squad meandered over from the water jug to where he was standing. Leo vaguely listened as they talked about how hard the run was, how they were getting better as a group, and other such things that squads spoke about after their morning workouts.

"Say, Leopold, do you want to get some water?" one of the people whose name Leo hadn't yet learned called. Leopold. That was what they had come to call him.

It was a strange name, and while he didn't hate the sound of it, it certainly wasn't his. Ever since he could remember he had been Leo, and as much as he appreciated the attempts at friendship, he would have liked it if they hadn't tried to change what he was called.

"No, I'm fine," he replied with a shake of his head.

Laughter echoed throughout the group and Leo's face reddened. What had he done to deserve that?

"Do you know how far we ran this morning, Leopold?" another unknown squad member asked.

He shook his head.

Another round of laughter echoed, only making Leo feel worse. He hadn't joined the squad to be ridiculed. He had wanted a purpose and the Captain had made it sound as though this was how he could find his in Dagsland.

Well, if this was what searching for purpose looked like in the village, then perhaps his theories of isolation hadn't been misplaced. Was it possible that the Captain had just wanted to give her squads someone to laugh at? A modern day jester?

If that was the case, then they would have to find someone else. Leo turned and just as he was about to leave, someone placed a hand on his shoulder. He whipped around, fists clenched, to find Barnes with a kind smile on his face. A bit of Leo's tension faded, and his lower lip wavered. He hadn't realized just how upset he had become, how angry their mockery had made him.

"We ran a marathon," Barnes said, "and you didn't even break a sweat. They're laughing at how incredible you are. And you are. Incredible, I mean. I've never seen anything like it."

A foreign feeling of warmth spread throughout Leo's chest as a smile tugged at his cheeks. A marathon? He could vaguely remember what that was, but not well enough to be able to tell how impressive that was. For the moment, though, he accepted his joy, he accepted his praise, and most of all, he accepted the group.

And if he had to be called Leopold to find more feelings like those, then so be it.

X

As the days went on, Leo's squad was beginning to make more of an effort to include him in things. While Drum didn't yet have any insults to throw at him, some of the other members of his squad did, and Leo was pleased to find that they didn't offend him.

Even so, he could tell that he wasn't fully a member of their team. If anything, he was a temporary inclusion to their more permanent roster. While it was true that they all worked out together, sparred together, and ate together, he was excluded from the one place where all of the bonding happened. The barracks. In this place, about which they complained endlessly, they all slept in the same room and often stayed up late talking and playing games. It was this time that made them a team, and Leo hated that he couldn't be a part of it.

As he was becoming more comfortable with the team, Leo began to consider asking the Captain if he could move into the barracks with them. He knew that people would say he was stupid for wanting to give up his house, but he didn't care. He wanted to feel connected to someone again. It had been too long.

He had begun working with the squad to discover his purpose and had been quickly reminded that he already had been burdened with one. He needed answers. His family was gone, and every moment spent with his squad rang sorrowfully through his memories. They were a false replacement. Was it wrong for him to want them all the same, to try to join them in the barracks so that they might learn to love and care for him the way that his late wife and daughter had?

However, much to Leo's surprise, he wasn't the only one feeling the weight of his living situation. One day, after what most of the squad considered to be a particularly grueling training session, Ford pulled him to the side to talk.

"You should ask the Captain to move you into the barracks with us," Ford offered. "If you want of course," he added quickly. "I know how nice it is to have your own place, but I really think it'd be good if you spent more time-"

"I've thought about it," Leo interrupted, knowing where the other man was going. "And I don't know. Maybe."

Ford seemed a bit crestfallen by this response. "We'd like to get to know you better, you know? We'd all enjoy having you come to live with us in the barracks. You'd really be a part of our squad." He paused, perhaps to consider if he had spoken too harshly. "You know?"

Leo sighed. "How about this?" Ford nodded eagerly for him to continue. "I try staying tonight, and we see how it goes. If you guys enjoy it, then I'll consider it, but if not, then we can stay the way that we are."

Ford beamed. "That sounds fantastic." His face settled into seriousness. "But Leopold, I want to be clear on one thing."

Leopold. There it was again. It wasn't his name, but strangely it didn't feel so wrong for Ford to be calling him that.

"What's that?" Leo asked.

"In my mind, you'll always be a part of our squad, no matter what."

Leo nodded and thanked him, then went on his way. Ford was a kind soul, and of course he would say that, but he didn't understand everything that was going on. They hadn't done anything wrong. Nobody in the squad was making him feel unwelcome.

It was his mind. It was the leftovers of his prior life. They were a plague that ate away at everything he knew that he could be, and no matter how hard he tried, he couldn't find a cure.

Leo felt like a ghost, wandering through the world with an impossible task ahead of him. Forever wandering, forever alone, forever angry. Maybe Tim had been right. Maybe there was something deeper happening, and he was a plaything for the gods. But it didn't matter. Not to him. To Leo, his life was still filled with that vague sense of purpose, and nothing could change that. Not friends, not family, not a job. Nothing.

And maybe that was just the way that things would be. Forever.

X

Somehow, the barracks were even more crowded than Leo had imagined. There were five bunk beds to fit all ten of the members of their squad, and they had been placed so close together that Leo was curious how they had even been brought into the room. Perhaps they had built them inside?

Leo sat on one of the top bunks, which was apparently less desirable than a bottom bunk, and hung his feet over the edge to match the stance of the other upper bunkers. The conversation started casually, much like the way it went around the water jug. It was lighthearted and easy, without much substance. Then, as the night went on, the larger group interaction broke into smaller conversations between three or four people each, taking a deeper turn.

However, even in this smaller and more controlled setting, Leo was finding it difficult to participate. Many of the people whom he spoke to bore the scars of winter, in the form of missing fingers and ears. He tried not to focus on the damage too much and instead paid attention to what they were saying. Karpov missed his dogs. Reuter spoke of her childhood on the beach. Only when the conversation landed on him did Leo believe that he was truly meant to hear what they had said.

"What about you, Leopold?" Karpov asked. "What was your life like before the end of the world?"

Reuter nodded eagerly, agreeing with her friend. "We hardly know anything about you," she said.

Leo paused and considered these two people. He hardly knew them. Up until just a few minutes ago, he would have considered them strangers. Even so, something about the barracks was making him feel trusting, so he decided he should tell them everything.

He told them how he barely remembered the world before it ended. How he imagined that he had had a wife and daughter, though didn't know their names or what they looked like. He explained how he woke up one day in the forest and then made his way to a cabin in the woods where he met a man.

"His name is Hank," he said. "You might know him."

When he said this, their expressions darkened.

"You met Hank?"

Leo nodded. "I lived with him for a couple of days. I don't know if I would've survived without him. He was good to me." He looked back and forth between Karpov and Reuter. "You know him?"

Karpov said nothing, but Reuter nodded ever so slightly.

"We know him," Reuter muttered while Karpov balled his hands into tight fists.

Leo could tell it was a tough subject, but his curiosity got the better of him. "How?"

Reuter shook her head and turned away to lay down and go to sleep. Leo looked at Karpov and noticed he had done the same.

Somehow, with just one mention of his late friend's name, Leo had killed a conversation. Feeling lost and confused, he tried to dissolve into the depths of sleep, only succeeding when the blackness of night began to glow with the coming of the sun.

X

Leo woke with a jerk, tearing him from the comfort of his bed. His back slammed against the ground an instant later, sending a dull ache through his body. He gasped for air and found none.

A fist connected with his face and another with his stomach. Leo tried to cover his head with his hands and was pummeled for his resistance. He cried and thrashed about. His foot went into someone's body with a thick crunch.

They screamed and began to hit him harder and faster. It was too much. Leo began crawling away, and they kicked his hands out from under him. It was too much.

Pain lanced through his head as the four different realities tried to show that they were the real one. In one he was crippled and broken. In another he had scored a few hits on his assailants but had been bested all the same. In the third he had escaped, just as he was about to in his current one.

But they had all happened. Somehow. They were all real. No, he had to keep going. Now wasn't the time. He had to escape or they would beat him harder.

It was too much. His mind couldn't handle it. The scars on his chest burned. With a crack, he felt his consciousness fade and his forehead hit the ground with a thud.

X

Leo sat in the Captain's room with a few other villagers that he didn't know. They glared at him as if he were a being of incomprehensible evil. How could they sit there and act like they hadn't just assaulted him while he was defenseless and sleeping?

He wanted to focus on their conversation. He really did, but his head hurt too much. At one point the Captain addressed him, and he just nodded as best he could. Strangely, he didn't feel very sore from the attack, and as he thought back to their strikes, none of them hurt nearly enough to bother him.

The discussion echoed around him as if he were hearing it through a thin door. Leo caught and understood every few words, and though it was a decent amount of information, he couldn't piece together anything meaningful about what had happened.

When the others left the room, Leo's head was swimming. He

had to have heard them wrong. Right? There was no way they had said what he had thought they had said. Leo opened his mouth to say something to the Captain, but no words would come. She shook her head sadly.

He left the room and returned to his cabin on the edge of town considering his options. What was he going to do? He could only remember two words from the conversation, and they scared him to no end.

Kill. Hank.

X

Tired, hungry, and alone, Leo wandered over to the dying flame upon which their pot of stew sat. He had watched from the side and waited for everyone to finish eating before he served himself out of fear of another attack. The last thing he wanted to do was divide Dagsland over something that he didn't understand.

They hated him now, he knew. It was hard to tell why. He assumed it had to do with Hank. The lumberjack was not an easy man to like considering all that Leo knew about him. Even so, he still considered the other man a friend. Somehow.

It occurred to him as he stepped closer and peered inside the stew pot that the same couldn't be said about the people of Dagsland. They were supposedly good people, yes? They were supposed to have welcomed him into their arms.

A tear streaked down his cheek, and he broke his wooden bowl between his fingers. Suddenly their brotherhood seemed so feeble. How could they say that they were better, that he was one of them, when they couldn't even have been bothered to leave him any?

X

Leo stood awkwardly amongst the ranks of the other villagers. Their hatred for Hank suddenly made infinitely more sense. He shifted uncomfortably within his loose-fitting combat garb. He was dressed exactly like the riflemen that had attacked Hank before.

They had been from Dagsland.

He didn't know what to do or what to say.

He understood their hatred.

Leo gagged as he thought about the stew. He could have ended up eating Ford, or Barnes. Maybe even the Captain if it came to that.

They were right to have beaten him. He would have beaten him, too.

Killing Hank wasn't going to change anything. Leo didn't want to do it. He didn't. Hank was his friend, no matter what. But if he could do something to ease the suffering of someone else, he would.

Out of the gates of Dagsland and with the other villagers he marched. To war, to glory, to salvation. Well, for them that was why they left. For him, it was to be seen, to be heard, to be felt.

For them it was a battle, while for him it was an apology. He just hoped he didn't have to be doing very much of the killing.

Dusk

The forest, as it always had and forever would, stood as a paragon of cold and dark. Just stepping past the gates of Dagsland sent a shiver down Leo's spine.

This was it.

He walked behind a stranger, careful to step where they had stepped. The Captain wanted to minimize their presence, and reducing the number of footprints they produced had been part of that. Leo took a deep breath, the frosty air burning his lungs.

He had betrayed his one and only friend.

They walked in single-file lines, with those in the lead wearing special glasses that allowed them to see at night. Nobody else had been given the privilege. Their group was silent, precise, and had a way about them that signaled the coming of death far more than Hank ever had.

How had he decided that these were the good guys, again?

Leo tried to think and was robbed of all clarity as the world split into three. A shriek, a murmur, and a whimper. He shook his head and tried to focus on the present. The splitting was coming more and more as of late, and he didn't imagine that it was going to stop anytime soon. He knew he needed to get used to it soon, but it was more difficult than it seemed.

He worried that he might lose himself in the memories of another, false reality. That one of the split worlds would grow so large and so prominent in his view that it would steal his mental clarity. That it would take him without warning, away from his life and his true self.

It was hard to tell what was true anymore.

The line came to a stop, and he almost bumped into the person in front of him. Leo shifted his vest uncomfortably, grimacing as it dug into his neck and armpits. It didn't fit him, and nobody had bothered to check. Well, maybe that was his fault.

They continued on a moment later, walking in the slow and methodical way that had marked their movement ever since leaving Dagsland. Why they did this, Leo didn't understand. He was sure that if they were to all make a beeline towards his friend's cabin, they would be able to eliminate him easily.

For this reason, he was grateful for the mistake that was their caution.

Up ahead, he heard a snap, a scream, and a squelch, in no particular order, and realized that he may have been mistaken. In the time it took for him to lose all confidence in their squad, the squad lost all confidence in itself and fell completely into chaos.

The line had broken. They had been walking for no more than a mile, and their system had already failed.

Just like that. With a snap, a scream, and a squelch.

X

It didn't take long for Leo to find the body. The rifleman lay in a heap within a single, taunting, pillar of moonlight. The corpse stank of blood and piss. Leo had no interest in spending any longer looking at the fallen soldier but remembered the men that he and Hank had fought and decided he should show some more respect.

Leo got down on one knee to examine the rifleman. With cold fingers, he pried off the man's helmet only to find that he wasn't a man.

He was a boy.

No older than fifteen or sixteen years of age, and he had already fought and died for his cause. Whatever that was.

Feeling numb, though unsure why, Leo stumbled away from the body as a question formed in his head.

Llooped

In all of his time in Dagsland, why hadn't he seen any children? Why was it only now that he was able to recognize the tragedy of the death of innocent youthfullness?

Everything hurt. Though his body was strong, Leo's mind was weak, so his soul bore the brunt of most of his suffering. It tore through him like a bullet through a man's chest, like an ax through a shirt.

Like his teeth through human flesh.

It was too much. The regret, the rage, the refusal to let himself believe that he had done something so horrendous all collided, deepening the cracks in Leo's mind. He fell to his knees and tried to be sick, but nothing came up. He hadn't eaten enough to do anything other than spit.

He took a moment to catch his breath and then noticed the sound of footsteps through snow. It was a soft crunch, not unlike how feet sounded on leaves, and when Leo looked up, he saw an unfamiliar looking man.

Though in the barest sense, there was something all too recognizable about him. It certainly wasn't his coloration, as Leo knew he had never seen anyone with hair that was so dark or eyes that were quite so black. It wasn't the knowing smile that covered otherworldly mysteries. It wasn't even the way that he vanished behind a thinner tree than should have been possible.

Leo couldn't put his finger on it, but even so, the man reminded him of Tim. Something about them was similar. In another world in which they had different eyes and hair, he could even imagine them being brothers.

| | |

Leo wandered through the forest, somehow managing to avoid all of the fatal traps. At one point a spiked log fell from a tree and threatened to impale his torso but he side-stepped and watched it swing uselessly .

His companions had not been quite as lucky.

Many of them had either fled or been killed since leaving

Dagsland. It was too dark to tell how or why they had met their respective fates, but Leo could practically taste Hank's influence in the air.

Somehow, he had known that they were coming. Somehow he had planned for them to attack in the way that they had, and somehow, he had been able to effectively stop all of them by himself.

Leo knew that the villagers hated his friend for his cannibalism, but there was no doubt that he was an incredibly impressive individual. Which made sense, considering how successful he was in his survival. Leo couldn't imagine how hard it would be to be able to live such a comfortable life in the dead of winter following the end of the world.

The memory of Hank lived bitterly within his mind. Leo wished he could come to a more stable consensus concerning his friend and worried what he would do were he to come in contact with the lumberjack again.

Behind him came the soft sound of footfall in snow. He spun in time to see a deranged man with a hatchet leaping towards him. Time was still, but Leo was not so constrained. He moved to the side and noticed then that it was Hank.

His friend had come to kill.

Leo backed away and waited until his perception of time returned to normal. "I won't hurt you," Leo said.

Hank spun on his heels and then made eye contact with Leo. "You're inhuman," he muttered. "Nobody can move that fast." He spun his hatchet in his hand and then darted behind a tree.

"Hank, you're my friend," Leo said as he raised his hand to his head. It was beginning to ache. "I wouldn't come out here to kill you."

Hank barked a laugh. "You're with Dagsland," he called. "Of course, you're here to kill me. Why else did you come? I'm not exactly nice to your people."

Leo balked. "My people? I've been with them for how long, and suddenly I'm one of them?"

"You're dressed like them. I'd be stupid to assume anything

else," Hank spat.

Now it was Leo's turn to laugh. "They never accepted me. Dagsland is a place to stay, but it's not my home. Your cabin, your fire, your friendship, that's where my home is. Not in their village."

A silence passed between them, and Leo worried he had said something particularly strange. It felt as if the tension that had built between them was fading with time, though Leo couldn't be sure that it wasn't just his imagination.

"Sometimes I miss having you around," Hank admitted, breaking the conjoined quietude. "I did appreciate your company."

Leo nodded in agreement even though they couldn't see each other through the trunk of the tree that Hank was hiding behind. Suddenly a splinter of pain shot through Leo's temple and the world began to pull itself apart into three disparate pieces.

They tugged at his mind, each begging Leo to accept it as his true reality. None of them were real. In one, he held a gun shakily and wandered through the woods, twitching at every minute movement within the shadows. They were all false. In another he carried a hatchet much like the one Hank carried. Someone was trying to trick him. In the third he walked unarmed, much like he did now, though Hank wasn't hiding behind a tree. Instead, in this third, Hank rushed to attack him. Leo flinched away and then remembered that he was imagining things.

"I wish you wouldn't have figured out about the stew," Hank continued.

Leo blinked and remembered their conversation. He could feel how close he had been to losing consciousness now, the dizziness taking hold.

"You would have had me live in ignorance?" Leo replied shakily.

"Better that than whatever they do in Dagsland," Hank chuckled.

Leo's head throbbed, and all of the pain from before returned with a vengeance. It was as if it needed him to sleep, to reset so that his body could adapt to whatever his ailment was. He didn't understand it but knew that no matter what, he needed to stay awake. He needed answers.

"Why did you do it?" Leo asked.

Hank snorted. "You wanna know?"

Leo paused to consider this. Did he want to know? Would it truly help him become a better person by understanding the motivations behind his friend who was a serial killer and a cannibal? After some intense, albeit brief, reflection, Leo concluded that he did.

"Tell me."

Hank didn't say anything for a moment. The ache in Leo's head persisted, distracting him far more than he would have liked. The images, as much as he hated them, grew stronger and stronger, taunting Leo with the possibility that they might be real.

As more time passed, Leo realized that he was starting to question whether or not one of the others was where his true consciousness was and this present one was the distraction.

"When you were a kid, did you ever play with bugs? Like ants, or beetles, or anything like that?" Hank asked.

Leo said nothing. He couldn't remember his childhood.

"I did," the lumberjack said. "Quite often, in fact. My parents thought I would become an entomologist. I knew just about everything about any bug that I found, from its native habitat to its favorite food. The problem was that my parents perceived my curiosity as love." He paused, and Leo thought he could hear the sounds of nails against metal. He was playing with the blade of his hatchet. "I think that's a dangerous assumption for them to have made.

"I didn't do it because I loved them. I didn't. They disgusted me. But more than anything, I was fascinated by just how different we humans were from them. How could we both be living beings with such different biology?"

Leo was confused and had no idea how any of this was relevant but refused to cut in. This was the most he had ever heard his friend speak.

"I wanted to know how they worked. Yes, I could read books

and ask my teachers at school, but I wanted to really know. So I started to trap bugs and pick them apart. Leg by leg, wing by wing, piece by piece, until I could see deep inside of them."

Leo frowned. The way Hank was speaking about it was discomforting.

"I didn't really learn that much by doing this, if I'm being honest," Hank said with a laugh. "I could see what they looked like but didn't have the know-how to translate that into any real findings. What I did discover, though, was that it made me feel good to do work like that. It made me feel really good.

"I liked the way that the bugs squirmed when I cut them. They were mine. I had control over them, and it was like their squirming was them begging for me to set them free."

He paused and Leo felt nausea creeping in. Maybe it was just from the headache. Hank wasn't a bad guy. Not really. He just did what he needed to.

"It wasn't long before bugs weren't enough. They became boring. Every time I trapped one, it was the same. I wanted something new, something that made me feel the same spark as the first beetle I cut open. So I upgraded to larger game.

"Mind you, it wasn't anything substantial at first. Just a few squirrels, a couple of rabbits, maybe a mole or two, and I learned that they, too, were incredible. However, like the bugs, they too became boring.

"At this point, I was in my late teens. Once my twenties rolled around, I went to college and it was harder to find time for my... indulgences. Still, after graduation, I started up again and found it harder to stop than before. Boars, dogs, anything at all that I could find and torture would tickle my brain in an inexplicable way.

"Until one day someone caught my eye. She was a woman, maybe a bit older than me, and I wanted nothing more than to cut her to pieces. The thought stuck with me for a while, though I never let it come to affect my actions because I knew it was wrong. Society had decided that it was wrong."

"It is wrong," Leo said firmly.

Hank stepped out from behind the tree with a dark glare. "I'm not done." He advanced on Leo as he twirled his hatchet between his fingers. "I waited for this girl, you see. As it turns out, I didn't have to wait long."

"The world ended," Leo muttered.

Hank nodded with a despicable grin. "Oh, yes it did. And with it went that society that liked to control me ever so much. I was lucky enough to find her before she died in some sort of accident, and just like that, I felt as though my itch had been scratched.

"Well, that was for a short time. I might have jumped the gun just a bit on when it would be safe for me to kill her," he said with a maniacal laugh. "Just a bit. The police came after me. Which was absolutely insane by the way. The world was ending, and they wanted to hunt down a murderer?

"Of course, my only real option was to run away. Which was how I came to find myself here, in this god-forsaken forest." He spread his arms and spun in a slow circle as he eyed the moonlit canopy. "But that's not what you wanted to know, was it?"

Leo took a slow step away from the lumberjack. "How do you go from that to eating them?"

Hank grinned. "And there's the million-dollar question." He paused and made a face of mock confusion. "Would it do to tell you that I didn't mean to? That I wanted to live out here in peace, and then I was found so I did what I could to ensure that I didn't starve? If I told you that, would you be satisfied?"

Leo shook his head. From what he had heard, that would be a lie.

"How about if I said that I'm insane? That I did it because the voices in my head told me that if I didn't do it, then I would go to hell?"

Again, Leo shook his head. "What are you getting at?"

Hank frowned dramatically. "Well, if it's neither of those things, then maybe we can deduce the truth." He grinned and dropped into a predatorial stance as if he were a snow leopard hunting Leo. "I wanted to do it. I liked it."

The lumberjack dashed forward with his teeth bared. The

smallest of giggles escaped his mouth just as he was about to swing his hatchet, and then the world froze.

Leo couldn't understand what was happening. Not truly. His friend and the man in the story that Hank had told couldn't have been the same person. It wasn't possible. Hank wasn't a bad man.

No, he was.

Leo's head pounded. Hank was the reason that he was still alive. The lumberjack had shared his food and shelter, even with no guarantee that Leo would be of any use.

Maybe he just wanted to torture and eat Leo.

Leo's chest burned in three ways, a pain beyond anything that he could reasonably endure. He keeled over and tried to parse through what he was seeing and feeling. Hank had been his friend, unlike the people of Dagsland. He had let Leo into his home and cared for him unconditionally, unlike the people of Dagsland. It was hard to imagine a world in which he didn't consider the lumberjack his friend.

And Leo knew him to be wicked all the same.

He rose to his feet and felt his mind snap. Reality had pulled too hard. All of the tugging, all of the confusion had amounted to too great a strain, and Leo was undone.

He was all four men at once. In one hand he held a pistol, watching the dead of night. There was a small flicker of movement in his peripheral vision, and Leo twitched his finger. The gun fired, sending a shockwave of energy through his arm and ejecting the empty bullet casing. It took him a second to realize that it had connected with Hank. The man had been stalking him.

Leo blinked and saw a hatchet buried into his friend's chest. He didn't know how it had gotten there. He let go of it with shaky hands and backed away, watching the lumberjack stumble to his knees with uneven breath.

He blinked again and saw his hand buried into his friend's body. Leo's forearm was wet with blood, and he could feel the slimy sensation of his friend's organs. With a flinch he pulled back, ripping his arm free and launching a layer of blood onto the snow.

Leo looked at his hand, and it wasn't covered in blood. Hank was still closing the distance, his face a malicious mess of mania.

"Don't get any closer," Leo cried.

Hank didn't stop his advance. He moved in slow motion, and Leo realized that he wouldn't be able to react in time even if he had heard Leo's cries for peace. So Leo walked towards his friend and placed his hand out to stop him. He couldn't run. Not now. Not after seeing his friend die so many times. If there were a way that he could end things and save the lumberjack's life, then he would take it.

As he was extending his arm, the first thing to make contact with Hank's body was his palm. It pressed gently at first, though Leo doubted it would stop the coming onslaught so he pushed a bit harder.

But instead of pushing the other man back, Leo's hand embedded itself into Hank's body. First it broke through skin, then it shattered bone, and then it shredded his internal organs.

Leo blinked and time returned to its normal pace. His hand was deep in his friend's chest, just as it had been a few moments prior. With a flinch he pulled back, ripping his arm free and launching a layer of blood onto the snow.

In four ways, Hank fell to the ground. It wouldn't be long until he passed. In all four worlds the great lumberjack that had saved Leo would be gone soon. Leo felt a lump forming in his throat. Was there anything he could do? He didn't know anything about medicine. All he could do was stand by and watch as his one and only friend took his last breath.

But most of all, Leo was beginning to consider that maybe he had done the right thing. And even with every justification that he could muster, telling himself that a cannibal and a serial killer needed to be removed from the world, Leo wondered about how much it still hurt to watch a dear friend die.

Did it make him evil to be sad to see evil go? Was he so bad that only Hank could accept him while everyone else saw him as the scourge that he truly was?

Leo sat and watched his friend for a long time, thinking about his place in the world. Tears came and went, screams echoed through the wood, attempts at resuscitation always resulted in failure, and nothing changed.

And deep down, there was something bothering him. He had taken someone's life before it was their time. Was he truly any different from the serial killer and cannibal? He had killed and hurt and eaten humans just the same as Hank.

Time passed with a slow gust of wind, pushing a cloud of mist through the forest. The trees which had been so clear and cold were now filled with fuzz and unfamiliar fury. The man that killed Hank was lost.

"I didn't mean to kill him," the man muttered. He squeezed his fists into balls. "I just wanted to protect myself."

Nobody was there to listen. Nobody was there to forgive him for his mistake nor to reward him for his success. Nobody was there to tell him that he had no reason to feel sad, nor were they there to shame him for not enjoying the glory of victory.

So he left, feeling the weight of loss. Another weight on his back, the burden no heavier than the others.

The man wondered about many things as he walked. First and foremost, he was curious as to how he had ended up in such a forest in the first place. It was dark, its majesty terrifying. He had no memory of his arrival. Secondly, he wished to understand his purpose. In his mind's eye, the man could see a girl, a woman, and now a man. The same man from before whose body had been left in the snow. Who were they? Why did he remember them? And finally, he wondered about the one phrase that was echoing through his mind.

It repeated like a song, filling him with hope. Its melody the only warmth in the cold forest. It was both new and old, fresh and nostalgic. The man held onto with all of the strength that his frail mind could muster.

"There is a place where you can find the answers you seek."

"Death"

Midnight

Before I continue and criticism is thrown at me like rotten food, I need you to understand my purpose in all of this. While I might be called the engineer of much of what happened, a parent of sorts, I don't feel as though this is as serious as you might believe. You, oh great God of Fate, who desires order within chaos.

I built my children to reduce our intervention. When we arrived, we sought to save so much, to fix all that was broken, and we stretched ourselves too thin. I built my children so that we may have more time for each other, so that we may rest.

So that we may no longer be so alone.

To Hythran I left this challenge. He is incomplete, as are all of my children, but in him I do believe strongly. I know that he has the capacity to correct this error, even though he and his siblings might make mistakes.

Yes, I know they caused this. They are not perfect. I just told you as much. Don't look at me like that. I never meant for them to become so rigid. You never approved, but you never would have. No amount of persuasion was going to change your mind. I didn't need your permission to create them, brother.

I did it for us.

Look at him now. Can't you see the hope within the hopelessness? His eyes are hollow and empty, but maybe that's better. Maybe now he can find the light with a clear view. Don't you ever wish for a fresh start?

He was given one.

Oh stop it.

It's not torture.

I can see his suffering as clear as you.

Won't you trust in Hythran, just this once?

I cannot talk to you when you get like this, brother. You are stubborn and old, and refuse to see when you might be wrong. This man could change everything for the better. You worry too strongly about what he will break. And yes, I admit, you could be right. He could be the end of everything.

You speak with such anger.

Take a step back.

Rcharyk, listen to me!

You read from the book of time and presume to know what is true, what should be. For your diligence, I thank you. But to what end must you toil?

We are eternity. We made sure of that when we arrived.

But perhaps that was a mistake.

Don't you ever wish that you could have a break from your duty?

I find that hard to believe. You've never once wished back to your days of adventuring?

I never thought I'd come to think of you as a liar.

Dreams of poverty often plague the minds of the rich. You are no exception.

If you'll just wait, I'll be done soon. Then you can go about your day, doing what you always do. But please, don't interfere here, and don't lose faith in me. I am trying to help.

Let's say he does break the world. Let's say he does this trip five times, six times even, and his Identity is so brutalized that neither you nor I can mend it.

The universe would end. We both know that. The very fabric of space and time would be shredded in an instant. Stars would be blown out like candles, and black holes would fall further into the nothingness of which they are harbingers.

We, too, would fade. And maybe that would be for the best. Perhaps this all came about because you and I are simply men.

Men that came into more power than we could have ever imagined and now need to rest.

X

The man of broken mind and shattered soul marched up the mountain with a powerful stride. He walked with the purpose of finding answers. The questions themselves were fading with each wayward snowflake, yet his purpose remained all the same.

He could feel the pull of the peak, its power incredible. Something stood at the top, something inexplicably strong that was calling to the man.

Perhaps this was where he would find the answers he so desperately desired.

Buried deep beneath this purpose was another, similarly deliberate ideal. Unlike the answers he so sought, this driving force was far simpler to understand. It was transparent in meaning and in cause. He wished to be free of his pain, of his regret.

He could feel a ceaseless amount of hatred in his heart. He wished it weren't so. He wished that he were happier.

Within his memories, something struck the man. There had been a time, not too long ago, that he had been happy. He didn't know why, nor did he remember anything of substance about the time, but he still did dream of the feeling. Of the happiness that had been like a blanket to shield him from the cold.

If only he could return to then. How much easier would his life be? Then he could get his answers without the hatred he carried. Then he could be unburdened in all ways.

The words of a god floated into his mind, and the man was reminded that he could find everything he wanted and more if he found a magical land. A land of magic. He frowned. Some part of him found that amusing. Magic didn't exist, did it?

Ever onward the man marched, the slope of the mountain his only companion. Sometimes his journey became blocked by ice, or obscured by stone, but he continued all the same, knowing that once he made it to the top all would be well. Once he was there, he could finally rest, and he would have everything for which he had ever wished.

| | |

The man could see the top of the mountain as clear as the morning sun. He could practically feel the power emanating from the top. It was thick like the winter's cold, its layers impenetrable.

Something incredible was going to receive him.

As the man marched ever closer, he started to hear breathing. Except this wasn't the sort of soft breathing one might hear from a sleeping babe. No, this was the breath of a beast, of a god perhaps, and even the small puffs of air that came from its lungs spoke of strength.

A flurry of snow and ice surrounded him as he took his ultimate step, marking his ascent to the peak. Shards of frost stung his skin and eyes as he tried to peer through the storm.

When it settled, there was a dragon sitting in from of him. It lounged as though it cared not for the man, though its gaze told another story. The dragon's eyes were green and sharp, as if they themselves could pierce a hole in the man's body.

"I am Hythran," the dragon said. "I am one of the gods of this universe, and I recognize your strength. For what is it that you wish?"

"I am allowed a wish?"

The dragon looked at him quizzically, though the man wasn't quite sure how he was able to read the beast's facial expressions. "That is why you came, yes?"

The man searched within himself and found this to be true, though he could hardly understand why. "I don't remember what I wanted from you," he replied.

Hythran snorted, and a cloud of snow blew into the man's face. "Never have I spoken with someone who is without a prepared wish. I do not know how to proceed. Perhaps you should take a moment and try to think."

So the man did as suggested and took a moment before saying

Llooped

anything. What did he want, now that anything was possible? Just a few moments ago he could have come up with such an easy answer, but now that the question had been posed, he found himself paralyzed by his options.

After some thought, the man decided that it would be best to resort to his feelings as his guiding light. But what was he feeling? Immediately, he noticed an ambient amount of curiosity. He knew there were questions whose answers remained unknown to him. How beautiful it would be to know everything, to be able to see behind every curtain he passed.

The idea seemed pleasant, if not a little boring.

Digging a little deeper, though, the man realized just how much a mistake it would have been to ask for answers. Beneath the surface, the man found a deep pain, one that he doubted he could ever understand. His ears rang with screams of agony. His stomach shook with nausea.

Now that he had noticed it, he couldn't get rid of it. The pain was to be his eternal companion, stalking him so that around every corner he turned, it would be there. Laughing, teasing, the past would always be there to haunt him.

With renewed resolve, the man squeezed his fists and stared deep into the dragon's dangerous eyes.

"I know for what I will wish," the man said through clenched teeth.

"And what might that be?" the dragon asked.

The man paused and felt some of the tension in his body leave. His fingers no longer seemed so attracted to his palm, his lower jaw relaxed. It would all be over soon. One more sentence, and he would be free.

"I wish I could do it all over again," the man said with a stark finality.

The dragon smiled, if such a thing was possible and then rose to its full height and spread its wings.

"Your wish has been granted," it said triumphantly.

The dragon reached one of its long, sword-like claws out and scratched the man's chest. The mark burned alongside three other similar scars he bore on his chest. A green light shone from the dragon's chest and fell upon the man's face. It was warm at first and then began to burn. The man turned away, shielding his eyes from the light, but it was too bright, too hot. So he decided to fight no longer. Perhaps submission was to be his only solace. With a breath, the man opened his eyes.

And then he saw everything.

| | | |

The world was cracked, but the man could see clearly. He saw a child standing in front of him, young and dark and beautiful. He tried to scoop her up in what he knew to be a familiar hug, but she disappeared before he could, replaced by a woman who looked just like her. Her face was stern, but sharp and smart, and the man knew that he was in love with her.

"I've missed you, Greg," she said before fading like the younger girl.

The man had no idea who Greg was, but he knew that he suddenly felt empty, except for the overwhelming regret that was coming over him.

He couldn't remember why he had wished for that. He thought he could feel himself hyperventilating, but perhaps it was just his imagination. He had wanted answers, not another chance at life.

Then the world cracked, breaking apart what little that he could see. Trees and snow fell first, but then people came into view. There were worlds that were made of steel and light, but soon even those things that seemed invincible broke away, leaving the man alone in the darkness.

Soon, the man was left with nothing to do or to think about. He could barely make out certain details, like his desire to find answers, but almost everything else was marred by shadows. Wind rushed from somewhere that he couldn't understand, ripping through the rags that covered his body. He could barely keep his eyes open. Just a moment of sleep would do. Just a moment...

A heavy weight settled upon the man as he became aware. His

name was Leo. He was lost. What else did he know other than loss? It was hard to understand. His head pounded and his chest burned. He lay his hand on the heat, and a strong sense of déjà vu washed over him.

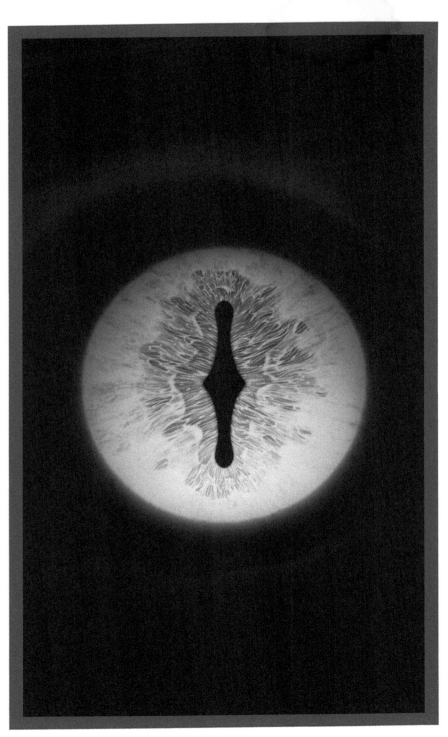

"Hythran"

Epilogue

Aervin watched from afar as the man struggled up the mountain. Power echoed around him like a shout into the void, yet of this fact the man seemed unaware. He walked as though he were weak and pathetic, lost and alone.

Broken and searching for salvation.

So there had been a reason that Aervin had been drawn to this corner of the universe after all. He tried to read the man's ka and understand the source of his strength but found something he had never seen before.

Most people were like books. You could read them linearly and learn about their life with ease. They were simple and uninteresting.

This man was different. Instead of having a single book which defined his life, he had five, and all of them were fighting for the opportunity to be read. None of them were long, though they were incomplete. It was as though someone had taken five different tomes, shredded them, and then glued them back together.

Not only that, but there was no clear beginning. The end merged into the beginning each time, and the first book had a shadow that stopped him from going any further back. How interesting. With a smile, Aervin flew to the man.

"Excuse me," Aervin said when the man didn't pay him any mind. Still nothing. Oh well, no harm in trying again. "Where are you going?"

The man looked up at him with empty eyes, and from the

closer distance, Aervin could make out streaks of frost that went from his eyes to his jaw.

The man stopped and stared at Aervin. "I'm going to the top," he muttered. "I need to go to the top." He looked away and continued trudging, shaking the ground with each mighty step.

"What's at the top?" Aervin asked as he floated cautiously after the man.

The man said nothing.

"What's your name?" Aervin asked, and this time something lit behind the man's eyes.

"It's…" He set his jaw and paused his ascent. To his credit, Aervin could tell that he was giving his best effort, though it likely wouldn't be enough.

So Aervin parsed through the mess of information that was the man's mind, seeking the closest thing he could find to an answer. The first word that resembled a name was Hank, though the man didn't look like a Hank, so Aervin searched deeper.

The second was the name Greg. Were Aervin to squint, then perhaps he could see the man being named Greg, but that was a stretch and names rarely had such vague applications. They were core to most people's Identities, and he imagined that even this man, with such a strange past, would be no different.

What stood out the most as being a possible candidate for the man's name was not a name but rather a collection of letters. In no particular order, Aervin saw the letters 'l,' 'l,' 'o,' 'o,' 'p,' 'e,' and 'd.' It took him a moment to realize what word these could form that was similar to a name.

"Leopold?" Aervin finished.

The man frowned and then nodded slowly. "Yes. Leopold sounds right to me." He turned and continued up the mountain, towards the well of power that Aervin was avoiding, the way someone might avert their eyes in the general direction of the sun.

"What do you hope to find at the top of the mountain, Leopold?"

Leopold shook his head helplessly. "Happiness," he answered, though the lack of confidence in his tone made Aervin wonder if it wasn't a question instead.

"Well you're in luck," Aervin said with a grin. "You can have happiness right now. Come with me, and you'll find all that you want and more."

Leopold furrowed his brow. Aervin hoped that the greed he felt hadn't corroded his words. He spoke with sincerity, ulterior motives aside. Yes, the man's strength would be nice to have, but he could also make Leopold happy.

"I don't know." He turned and pointed at the peak. "You're sure that you can give me what it can't?"

Aervin could tell instinctively that mere persuasion wasn't going to work very well on Leopold. The minds of the vacant were so challenging to entice that mere words wouldn't do. He would have to speak into the man's heart directly to alter his present fixation.

Deeper this time, Aervin searched into Leopold's Identity. What he was looking for, Aervin didn't have a clue. It just had to be important, to be manipulatable.

And then, in the depths of a bloody darkness, Aervin found something that almost made him feel sorry for what he was about to do. It was a longing, much like he had been expecting from Leopold, though not for what Aervin had been expecting.

Leopold didn't want money nor fame. He didn't want power, which was obvious seeing as how strong he was. No, he wanted something much simpler.

He wanted friends.

So Aervin put on his friendliest smile and began to scam the simple-minded fool that was Leopold.

"You know, I've been looking for a companion," Aervin started.

Leopold's face lit up. "You have?"

Aervin nodded casually. "Just someone I know I can rely on. You now how hard it can be to find someone like that these days."

"It really can be hard," Leopold agreed.

Aervin looked at Leopold intently and then shrugged. "Well,

if you happen to know anybody like that, let me know. It can get awfully lonely sometimes."

Leopold seemed to consider Aervin's words and then slowly opened his mouth. "I think I would like to go with you, if you wouldn't mind."

Aervin looked at him with mock suspicion. "Are you sure?"

Leopold nodded furiously. "As sure as I've been of anything in my entire life."

Aervin paused and tried to appear hesitant. "Well, if you really think that you'd like that, then you can come along."

The other man cheered, and Aervin picked him up with his ka and flew them away from the mountain. Aervin felt a wave of relief wash over him as they left. They had gotten dangerously close to the peak.

"I'm your friend?" Leopold asked feably.

"You're my friend," Aervin reassured him with a smile as they soared through the clouds.

Leopold grinned back, and Aervin took them to his home. There, he could save Leopold. There he could use Leopold. There, the two of them could work together, Aervin as the brains, Leopold as the brawn, and the world could finally change.

Acknowledgements

I first had the idea for *Llooped* directly after I finished *Annihilated*, back in 2021. The character, Leopold, was a mystery to me. I knew that I wanted him to have a strong body and a weak mind, but I couldn't think of how exactly I wanted to approach the problem.

The book went through a few iterations in my head, as they usually do, but this book proved to be particularly challenging for me. Perhaps this was because of the length, seeing as it is the shortest book I've ever written, or maybe it was the pressure that I put on myself to give Leopold the best origin story I could think of.

Regardless, after deciding that I didn't want him to be traveling to another planet, I decided that I needed to write another prequel to explain the prequel that was *Llooped*. That became *A Legacy of Pain*, which is an unpublished novel that explains the events of *Llooped*, and the original versions of *Annihilated* and its sequel. This book became a guide for me, leading me to write *Llooped* in the form that you found while reading this.

I finished the first draft of *Llooped* in 2022. Needless to say, I wasn't satisfied with what I had written. The writing felt sloppy, the story choppy, and it was a bit more amateur than I would have liked. The idea of publishing it made my skin crawl, so after having a friend read it and give me some feedback, I put it away, knowing that I would return to it in the future.

At this point I went to college and my world changed. Of course, it did, but in this case I mean that I didn't have enough time to be writing as much as I would have liked. I wrote two more novels in my first year but felt as though I should have been doing more.

Yes, writing is my passion, but publishing is how I express growth and mastery. So even with me writing as much as I was, I felt hollow and unfulfilled, like I was leaving my dreams behind.

To quench this thirst, I published a short story collection, which you can now read, called *Voices and Visions*. But as I was publishing this, it didn't feel as good as it usually does. For those that haven't read it, I ran a short story contest and published the winners in this book. The book was mine, but the stories weren't. I loved the process yet thought nostalgically on the days of when I was publishing my own books.

Which brings me to this book. A little under a year after publishing *Voices and Visions*, I see this hole in my life and know that I should fill it. A couple of weeks ago I told my friends that I needed this, and they told me I should pursue it. So I am approaching this with the fervor that I always do.

This will be the first book of three that comes out this summer.

Thank you to everyone that has supported me through this process. Most of all, thank you to my mother for being my editor and number one fan. I know we sometimes argue about the semantics of a sentence, but I can always count on you to help me realize my vision.

Printed in the USA
CPSIA information can be obtained
at www.ICGtesting.com
CBHW030636120724
11461CB00011B/301

9 781958 401026